AN ASSASSIN'S
PATH

AN ASSASSIN'S PATH

PATH

Secrets, Betrayal, and War

Kaylah Keys

To order additional copies of this book, contact:
Xlibris
844-714-8691
www.Xlibris.com
Orders@Xlibris.com
813351

CHAPTER ONE

Thunder boomed across the field, the rain was cold and felt like ice piercing her skin. Akatila looked across the field toward the enemy. She knew today was the day they had all been waiting for, today would decide what happens. Chezuv stepped forward beside her. He placed his hand on her shoulder and nodded to her. She shifted and took her stance. Out of the shadows came the others. Yukia stood beside her while her sister Angelia was on the other side. Everyone knew what they were ready to sacrifice. Chezuv shifted into his wolf and howled as they knew that was the order. They all ran across the field. Akatila counted everyone just to make sure everyone was there; however, when she counted, there was someone missing, but she could not figure out who. Everyone shifted back to their human forms.

"Move!" Chezuv nudged her.

"Chezuv, someone is missing!" she growled.

"We will figure out who soon. For now, we need to focus on winning this battle," he reminded her.

She nodded as she picked up her pace. Catching up to the others, she saw the look her sister gave her, and Akatila could only shake her head yes in hopes it would ease her sister. She saw the enemy was still coming over the hill and down into the field. She got an idea. She shifted into her fox form and whimpered to her sister and Harnuq. They shifted also and ran to her as she led them away from the fighting. They ran through the small thicket and waited. They remained low on the ground and out of sight. She saw Chezuv was close to the enemy and she nodded. They surprised the enemy from the side, crashing into them. Harnuq crashed into three soldiers while Angelia took out two. Akatila had a solider in her sights, but she saw something off the corner of her eye that made her stop.

"Get out of the way!" Malinter screeched.

He knocked Akatila to the side, taking the hit from the solider she was after. She shook her head, feeling the anger rise in her. She lunged at the solider, knocking him away from Malinter, and she bit down on his neck, making him wail. She felt someone tug on her tail. When she turned around it was Yukia. She sighed with relief. She chased the solider off before turning back to Yukia, who was gone again. She dug her claws into the ground and knew something was not right. She then saw General Miko and his son Miko Jr. She growled and went to attack, but Chezuv stopped her and shook his head at her. They both shifted and looked at each other, Akatila was furious.

"We won this field, do not go after them. You know that you will not win. They will kill you on the spot. Give it time, fight by fight," he whispered to her.

"Where is Yukia?" she asked coldly.

Chezuv looked around, and to his surprise, the young man was nowhere on the battlefield. He looked back at Akatila but she was already furious, and he knew this would not end well. They searched for the others and everyone was accounted for except Yukia. She turned to her sister when she noticed her sister's eyes were wide. She glared, looking behind her to see their old friends who'd turned on them leaving them for dead years ago. She growled, shifting immediately, and chased after them. Angelia was right behind her and Harnuq was beside her. Akatila made it to a small clearing. Her sister and Harnuq went after the others. She was face to face with someone she never thought she would see again. She growled coldly as she had hoped this time would be different. Akatila shifted into her human form and narrowed her eyes glaring coldly at her.

"Miss me?" she snickered.

"Trust me, Nakamyomi, no one misses you," Akatila spat.

"So rude. Some things never change, huh, Akatila? Hey, by the way, where is Yukia at?" she snickered.

Akatila shifted quickly and went to lunge at her, hoping to get her claws in her. However, she was hit from the side by someone. She hit the ground tumbling, slamming her head against a boulder. She tried to focus on the figure who attacked her. Her vision was blurry but she knew the scent. Her heart shattered and questions swirled in her head, until she smelled someone else. She became nervous. *Oh, Angelia, where are you? Please hurry,* she thought to herself.

"Get away from her!" the voice growled, stepping in front of her to protect her.

"Traitor!" Nakamyomi screeched.

Her screech brought everyone running. However, by the time they got there Nakamyomi and the mystery guy were gone. Akatila could still smell the other stranger. She did not feel the need to be afraid for some reason. He gently picked her up and brought her to where everyone was. They had been looking for her. Akatila's head was bleeding slightly. It looked bad for the newcomer as no one knew who he was, where he had come from, why he was there, if he had caused this or saved her.

"And you would be?" Angelia said, stepping out of the shadows along with Harnuq.

"My name is Rikunamora, Riku for short," he said calmly.

"And who did this to my sister? Did you, do it?" she asked, becoming hostile.

Ze ran over. He grabbed Akatila from the stranger and took her to Shala's tent. Ze sat her down and Shala began to address her wound. Akatila tried to speak, however she couldn't so she pointed at the newcomer, and Shala could tell she knew something. She ran over and stepped between them, which made Ze get up as well. He stood by the tent where Akatila was but he never lost sight of Shala either. Shala put her hand gently on Angelia to get her attention while Riku had gone silent seeing Shala. He knew better as he saw Ze glaring at him. He bowed his head to Shala in respect, figuring she was the medicine healer for them. He took a few steps back. Angelia looked to Shala with confusion.

"Listen to me, Angelia. I know you want to know what happened, but I can tell you right now he was not the attacker. The attacker left his scent on her and it does not match this young man's. There is also a faint scent from a female. Any ideas?" Shala asked softly.

"Nakamyomi, as for the other attacker, I have no idea," she replied, trying to think.

Ze saw that Akatila was trying to get up. He went in and helped her to her feet. He wrapped one arm around his shoulders so she had leverage. He helped her out of the tent and to the others. Shala quickly ran to her to make sure she was okay. Chezuv and Malinter stepped forward along with the others. Chezuv knew Akatila knew the attacker.

"Akatila, tell us what happened," Chezuv said kindly.

"I saw Nakamyomi. I went after her. I wanted to get revenge because she had attacked Angelia a few months ago. However, she led me to a clearing of some sort. I did not scent anyone else with us, just me and her. When I went to lunge at her, I got hit from the side. I tumbled to the ground and hit my head. I could not see the attacker. I knew him though, I knew the scent. And if it were not for this man, I really think the other guy would have let Nakamyomi kill me," Akatila replied.

"So he saved . . . you?" Angelia said embarrassed.

"No worries about being hostile, she's your sister, right? I get it, siblings are very protective over each other. As for the attacker, I know Nakamyomi very well. She is a traitor and should not be trusted," Riku declared.

Everyone looked at Riku with surprise on he spoke of Nakamyomi, but they nodded in agreement. They knew that the young woman was a danger and would never be trusted. Chezuv stepped forward and spoke quickly.

"Harnuq, you, Anoquv, Sprin, Malinter, Shala, and Ze, head back to camp and make sure that things are okay there. Make sure we did not get hit on two fronts," he said calmly.

Harnuq, Anoquv, Sprin, Malinter, Shala, and Ze made their way back to house. Angelia stayed with Chezuv, Angelia, and Riku. Chezuv looked at him as he knew that he could trust him, he just could not say how he knew. He nodded to Akatila and Angelia both. Akatila smiled and sighed in relief. Angelia was not convinced yet. She knew it would be some time before she fully trusted this man, especially around her sister.

They all returned to the courtyard—that is what they called home for now. Riku looked around and Akatila could tell he was uncomfortable. She nudged him gently and smiled, making him relax. The courtyard was a huge opening surrounded by a beautiful gray-and-black high rock wall. There were fifteen different little houses on the edge of the courtyard and a huge willow tree in the middle of the yard that looked like it had been there for centuries. Riku took it in and smiled before looking to Akatila and chuckled lightly.

"This place is so nice, better than the forest," he muttered.

"It's home for now," she said softly.

Chezuv stood up on the tree stump beside the willow tree and called for everyone to gather around. Akatila figured that it was going to be about the battle and to talk about what was going to happen to Riku. She hoped that Chezuv would let him stay with them. She was curious about him and drawn to him for some reason.

Chezuv waited for everyone to gather and finally after a few minutes everyone was around the stump.

"Everyone knows we won the battle. However, with that we did lose someone. Yukia is now missing. Keep an eye out for him, he may have been taken by the enemy. Also, we have a new member joining us, Riku," he said carefully.

"Are you sure we can trust him?" Harnuq asked.

"He will prove himself. He will train with us, earn our trust. But for now, yes, he is to be treated fairly until given a reason not to," Chezuv stated.

Everyone nodded except Angelia, who was still glaring at him. She did not trust him whatsoever. She was still convinced that it was he who attacked her sister. Her eyes remained narrowed as Akatila stepped forward.

"Chezuv, may I train him?" she asked.

"What! Akatila, are you serious?" Angelia exclaimed.

"Yes," Chezuv replied to her.

Angelia growled, turning her back to Riku and her sister. Akatila sighed softly before looking to Riku with a gentle smile. Akatila knew that Angelia was just being protective, but she also knew that there was something special about him and she was going to find out.

"We start later today." She smiled before walking off.

Sprin had stepped forward to show the young man around the camp. He made sure to show him his own little house. Riku had followed Sprin to the very edge of the line of houses. They came to a small little house, simply perfect for one person. Akatila came out of the house to the right and she smiled at him before walking to her sister and Harnuq, who were waiting for her.

Riku entered his new home and got settled. He decided to take a quick nap before his first training sessions. He woke up later that day. He jumped out of the bed and ran out to the courtyard. He noticed Akatila was training with someone and he decided to wait. He watched the way she moved and how she never lost composure. He felt someone nudge him and he turned to see Chezuv standing beside him. Akatila came running over as she won her match. He nodded to them. Chezuv knew that Riku's training had finally begun with Akatila. She giggled gently as they got to the middle of the courtyard. She placed her hand on her *katana* and tossed it to the ground. He looked at her confused.

"Hand to hand first until you get your katana," she giggled.

"I do not want to hurt you," he said softly.

She laughed softly, which caused everyone to gather on the grass. They wanted to watch someone finally beat Akatila hand to hand. Even Chezuv and Malinter were in the courtyard watching.

"Seems we have an audience," he said shyly.

"Well, start. Attack me," she said, ignoring everyone.

He nodded and took a stance. He exhaled and ran at her, swinging his arm, attempting to punch at her. She ducked under him and tripped him with her foot. He tumbled onto the ground but he was able to grab onto her, making her fall as well. She let out a small huff as she tumbled. She tumbled with him and ended up pinning him. She snickered softly. He groaned before batting her in the face to distract her and cause her to lose balance. He then quickly knocked her off him. She groaned and got to her feet, but his hand was by her throat. She bowed to him in defeat. Everyone cheered.

"Congratulations, no one had ever been able to trip me up like that," Akatila giggled.

"You were probably going easy on me," he teased.

She gave a small smile before returning to her sister and Sprin who had been waiting for her. Sprin kept laughing as he loved the idea of someone finally winning against Akatila.

"Sweets, you finally lost!" Sprin smiled.

"Sweets?" Riku said confused.

"It is a nickname I have had all of my life." Akatila replied softly.

They each went their own ways as they each had chores to get done, Chezuv watched them and knew that things would work out. Angelia finally came around to having Riku around as she saw how happy he made her sister. She could not hold what Yukia had done against Riku, Yukia left Akatila and Riku saved her. She sighed as she approached Riku.

"Riku? Do you have a moment?" Angelia asked.

"Oh, um of course." He said nervously.

"I wanted to apologize to you. I was trying to protect my sister. After the battle and Yukia leaving her behind, I did not want to see her hurt again. But I understand now that you are not here to hurt her, you saved her and brought her back to me. Thank you." She said bowing her head slightly.

He stood there shocked, but returned the gesture as she walked off, he returned to his home and laid down. He knew that he would do whatever it took to keep everyone here safe, he had finally found a home.

A few months had gone by since the battle and everyone had come around to Riku being in the group. He fit in very well and he and Akatila became remarkably close very quickly. They were inseparable. Angelia watched them as they hung out underneath the old willow tree in the courtyard. She gave a soft giggle. She knew it was only a matter of time. She noticed Chezuv talking with Malinter. She snuck her way over and ease dropped as her curiosity got the best of her. She still could not here them, but she had a guess on what they spoke about. There had been rumors of a new threat in the forest, Angelia was dying to know who or what it was, but she had to be sneaky about it.

She became curious, however, about who the new enemy that was crossing into the forest was. Angelia waited until nightfall to make her move. She snuck out of the courtyard and headed straight into ShadowCry Forest in excitement and concern. She had no idea what she might find.

After she ran for a bit, she came across some tents. She stuck to the shadows and shifted into her lynx and tried to stay out of sight. The shadows gave her great coverage, or so she thought. She heard footsteps behind her, she did not dare to shift back to herself.

"Well, well, well, what do we have here?" she heard someone say from behind her.

"No need to shift, we know you belong to the Chezuv traitor group. We can smell it on you. So why don't you tell us why you are here?" the solider snickered.

Angelia knew to run, so she did. She charged past them, running back into the forest. She knew she would lose them as she knew the forest better than any intruder could ever hope to know. She made it back to camp to find Akatila standing at the gate glaring at her. She shifted back to herself and smiled at her sister. She went to walk past Akatila, but she grabbed her arm quickly and brought her back in front of her.

"And where did you go so late at night?" she glared.

"I could not sleep, so I went for a run. Who made you gatekeeper?" Angelia replied, lying.

Akatila said nothing else as she knew her sister was lying, but she would not try and force it out of her. She shook her head and returned to the fire pit. She sat beside Riku, who gave her a soft blanket and wrapped her up in it, chuckling at her. She felt herself blush when she noticed Chezuv was looking at her. She got up and walked over to him out of curiosity. She looked up at him and sighed, knowing what he was going to ask. She could not believe her sister would lie, and she was about to get the scolding for it.

"I have no idea where she went, Chezuv. Knowing her, to find out who the intruders are in the forest. She said she went on a run and left it at that," Akatila spoke softly.

"Akatila, we need her to understand she just cannot run off and do these things by herself. What if she had been caught? We would have never known about it until maybe it was too late," he replied harshly.

"Get some sleep, Akatila. We go into town tomorrow, remember." He smiled at her.

She nodded and went back to her little home. She gave a wave goodnight to Riku who was entering his home as well. She saw her sister. As Angelia smiled, Akatila turned away as she just got scolded for her sister's mistake again. She entered her home and laid on the bed and sighed. She had no idea what her sister was thinking or why she would run off like that. Akatila let out a groan. She placed her hand over her eyes in annoyance. She turned over and closed her eyes. Despite her sister's actions, she was excited to go to the market in the morning. She had hoped to find new rope for her katana. She finally drifted off to sleep.

The sunshine came through, beaming her on the face. She felt the warmth and giggled gently as she yawned. She stretched and got to her feet. She knew it was the day for the market. She quickly got dressed and ran into the courtyard. Riku was awake, so were Sprin and Angelia. No one else was up yet. She huffed, knowing they had to wait for everyone else. She smirked, looking to Sprin.

"I bet we will make it to town before you!" Akatila teased.

"In your dreams, Akatila, I will win this time," Sprin replied, smirking.

"Didn't you say that last time Sprin?" Angelia questioned.

"Hey, you stay out of this!" He pouted.

"Woah Sprin no need to be all grouchy." Harnuq chuckled coming from the house.

Akatila and Angelia both started laughing until they saw everyone else start coming out and they knew it was finally time. They jumped to their feet, made a mad dash to the gate. Everyone began walking to the town and everyone was talking and having a great time. Akatila and Angelia saw the entrance to the town and ran off, leaving Riku and Sprin behind. But Riku caught up to them.

"Hey, you three, wait for me!" Sprin shouted as everyone made their way to the town.

"You're just too slow, Sprin!" Akatila teased.

As everyone got what they needed, Sprin, Akatila, Angelia, and Riku ran throughout the town. Malinter was the first one to find something. He took it to Chezuv and asked about it. Chezuv nodded to him and Malinter went to find Akatila.

CHAPTER TWO

"Wait up! Akatila, Angelia, Riku!" Sprin yelled as he chased after them.

They ducked and dodged people in the market square. Akatila looked back to see Riku right behind her while her sister, Angelia, was on her right side. All three came to a stop as they almost crashed into Malinter. He was holding onto someone behind him. Angelia and Sprin both knew exactly who it was as they had caught the scent, but Akatila was too focused on Malinter to notice.

"Uh-oh," Akatila muttered as she looked up at Malinter and saw his look of annoyance.

"Must you four always cause trouble?" he asked, seeing Sprin running around the corner.

Everyone looked down at their feet except Akatila. She kept Malinter's cold gaze until she saw Yukia pop his head from around him. She glared at him. She rolled her eyes and went to leap at him but Riku grabbed her gently. Her gaze was cold as she turned her back to him. The young man shrank back as he was not sure why she hated him so much. She smiled back, looking to her sister, Sprin, and Riku before feeling a hand on her shoulder. Malinter turned her around to face Yukia. He then remembered that Yukia left her on the battlefield. Malinter had hoped she would have forgotten about that. The hostility in her eyes told him that she had not forgotten and she hated him for it. However, the guy beside her, Riku, caught Yukia's attention as he did not know him, and there was a feeling of jealousy that arose in him. He kept silent for the time being as Malinter looked as if he was going to snap at Akatila. He knew better than to start something at that moment.

"Akatila! Do not turn your back on me. You are going to accept that Yukia is back with us now and you will treat him with respect! And due to your interest in him, you are going to be the one whom he trains with." Malinter glared at her as his cold words pierced her, which made her blood boil.

"What! Why me? I have no interest in someone like him! Make one of the others do it. The girls in camp will drool over him anyways! He will only get hurt if he trains with me. And I am not explaining his injuries to Chezuv or to Shala! He is a traitor! He left us at the battle! He should not be here, he does not belong with us anymore!" she was quick to snap back, glaring at Yukia. Seeing him shrink back only made it worse.

Riku, Angelia, and Sprin did not like this plan as they all knew why Yukia wanted Akatila to train him, but Akatila was clueless of it. Riku glared before stepping beside Akatila, placing his hand gently around her waist, smirking at Yukia. Yukia noticed and his mood changed as he stepped from around Malinter, facing Riku. Yukia's normal gentle green gaze turned dark as his mouth slightly parted.

"And who are you exactly!" he snapped at Riku.

"Name's Rikunamora. Riku for short," he replied, still holding on to Akatila gently.

Akatila let herself relax as she knew Riku would not let anything go wrong; however, when she relaxed, she noticed Riku pushing himself a bit closer to her. She glanced down, only then noticing his hand was around her waist and she smiled a bit before looking back up to see Yukia close to them. Yukia never looked to Akatila as he gave a low growl and his eyes turned a dark green. Akatila noticed Riku's normal green gaze was turning blue, and she knew what was about to happen. She quickly turned in front of Riku, blocking Yukia from getting to Riku.

"Riku, do not do it. He is still a newbie. You will hurt him and it will be me getting in trouble for it. I have no choice but to look after him now. It came from Malinter, which means it came from Chezuv. Please calm down," she begged him softly.

"You know why he chose you. Everyone gets a choice, Akatila," he replied softly but his voice was still cold.

"Riku, please," she whimpered looking up to him.

He looked down at her and sighed. His eye color returned to green and he relaxed. However, he bent down and gave her a soft kiss. He pulled her to him and deepened the kiss before she finally pulled back. She said nothing but she looked down from his gaze. She then turned to Yukia and knew that if she fought this it would make things hard, but she noticed he had not calmed down. She glanced back to Riku and gave a slow nod and he left. She looked back to Yukia, who was now looking at her. She knew she had to play nice, she looked at him for a moment, getting a good look. She had forgotten exactly how tall he was. He stood around 6'2". He was very toned but he was also still very slim. His black hair barely was long enough to start covering his eyes. She moved her hand slowly to his face. He glared but he relaxed a bit. She smiled and moved his hair out of his face. He relaxed fully, and his dark green eyes returned to being a soft green. He gently pulled her to him, her body completely against his, her hands gently placed on his chest.

"I am sorry for how I acted, Akatila. I chose you because you are the best assassin out of the whole camp. I just wanted to learn from the best," he said softly.

"Well, picking a fight with my best friend is not the way to start things off, Yukia. I must learn to trust you all over again after you left during the battle. If it were not for Riku I would have died," she said, looking up to him.

She felt his heart race. She sighed and hugged him. She felt his grip tighten on her softly as he embraced the hug. From the trees Riku was watching, making sure she was safe as he did not trust Yukia. But he was distracted by Angelia, while Sprin remained a bit further back.

"My sister loves you, you know that. She will never say it because she does not know how to. But you should not be quick to judge Yukia. Yes, he left but he is back now. It is you that Yukia should not trust. You appeared in that battle out of nowhere and saved her. I still do not know why you are here, where you came from, or what you plan to do. But my sister seems to trust you. Do not ruin that," Angelia said to him, looking at her sister with Yukia.

Akatila pulled out of the hug and smiled at him before turning away. He followed her as they both ran toward camp. Riku, Sprin, and Angelia followed them. Akatila glanced behind her to see her sister, Sprin, and Riku, and she smiled. It felt like old times again before the war, just with a new friend.

They got back to camp laughing and talking. That was when they saw a general in the middle of the camp. Yukia and Riku both quickly jumped in front of Akatila, while Angelia ran to Harnuq and Shala. Sprin remained standing by the entrance of camp, guarding it just to be safe. Chezuv finally stepped out of the house, facing this man with Malinter on his right and Ze on his left.

"What can we do for you, General Miko?" Chezuv spoke firmly.

"One of your own, Chezuv, was found sneaking around our camp last night. I am not sure on who exactly, but here is my warning. If I catch any of your students sneaking around again, I will kill them. Do you understand?" the General replied harshly.

Akatila thought to herself, "*None of us have been in that camp. Who could he be talking about?*" She shook the thought from her mind and focused on what the general was saying. Shala, Anoquv, and Sprin finally came from the front gate, another person following them. Akatila turned around to see who it was. When she saw Raynier, her heart raced and her breathing picked up. Yukia glanced back because he felt her grip tighten on his kimono, and he saw Raynier. Her gaze widened at the sight of him. She thought he was dead and now he is standing in front of them all. Riku glared at Raynier, but Raynier's gaze was locked on Akatila. She met his gaze finally and she ran to him. She did not even think about it. Riku and Yukia both went to grab her but she managed to slip past them. Raynier extended his arms, embracing her once again. She felt her body tremble as she tried not to cry at seeing him again. He wrapped his arms completely around her and held on to her. He sighed softly as if he was relaxing, seeing her again. She pulled back for a moment and looked at him. He had new scarring that was never there before. She then realized it was Angelia who had been almost caught only because she heard the general's description.

"Chezuv, she was about 5'7", brown hair, green eyes, and young. If anyone with this description is . . ." The general stopped in midsentence once he saw Angelia.

Akatila looked to Raynier. He closed his eyes and she realized he was shielding her from the general's sight. He was trying to protect her yet again, but this time she would not let anyone take the fall for it even though Angelia was the one who caused the trouble. Harnuq tried to get to Angelia before the general, but Akatila was able to get away from Raynier's grip. She cleared her throat, which made the general turn around. Harnuq was able to sneak Angelia out of camp. He approached Akatila slowly. He glared at her as she stood her ground. Raynier tried to jump in front but was held back by another soldier.

"So it was you. Sneaking around, looking for a new way to try and stop us, huh? Or trying to see your lover?" the general said, seeing how Raynier was acting.

"I do not have one, sir, but I was simply curious. I had never seen you this close and my curiosity got the best of me," Akatila said, lying.

"Well, guess what? Now you get to see the main camp firsthand! Raynier! Get her out of here now!" the general spoke harshly.

Raynier came up to Akatila and sighed gently, grabbing her arm, and taking her out of the training camp. Chezuv did not move as he knew it would not matter. With the way the war was going, he could not save her, not yet.

Akatila said nothing as she left; however, Yukia and Riku both tried to run after her. Angelia was right behind them. Harnuq pinned Angelia down while Malinter grabbed Yukia, and Sprin grabbed Riku. Angelia cried as she watched her sister be taken for something that she did not do. Harnuq held on to her as she finally submitted and relaxed in his arms. Everyone sat there on the ground except for Shala, Ze, Chezuv, and Anoquv. Everyone was speechless at what just happened. Angelia broke free from Harnuq and ran to Chezuv. He looked at her with pity in his eyes as her eyes were red from crying.

"We both know it should be me! We both know she did nothing wrong! Tell the general he made a mistake! She cannot get taken for this! They will hurt her!" she pleaded.

"She is safe as long as Raynier is there. He will not let her get hurt. He loves her too much for that to happen. Until we figure out a plan to get her out, she has no choice, and we can only hope nothing happens to her or Raynier," Chezuv said calmly.

Riku glared looking to Yukia as he did not trust him. Yukia looked unfazed by the fact Akatila was being taken away. He looked guilty of something. Riku wondered if Yukia was going after Akatila, or Raynier. He went to approach Yukia. Sprin stepped between Riku and Yukia, breaking his line of sight. Anoquv and Harnuq also stepped beside Spin; all three of them shook their heads no to him.

"He knows something, I know he does. If he is the reason Akatila is being taken, I will kill him myself. He is not to be trusted. I do not care if he is your brother or not, Sprin," Riku said before turning away from them.

Sprin stood there glaring at Yukia, he wondered why Yukia was back and where had gone. He knew his brother, but this man he looked at was not Yukia. Sprin looked at Chezuv and shook his head no before leaving to find Riku.

Raynier gently held on to Akatila the entire way to the main camp. They walked through ShadowCry Forest and into the main camp, which was located on the edge of the forest beside the Red River. She sighed, but she felt Raynier's hand gently on her hip letting her know she would be okay. She gave a nod and followed them into the prison. There, she was thrown into a cell and the door slammed shut. A few days had gone by she heard the door open, she thought it was Raynier. When she looked up it was a large guard standing there. She tried to get away from him, but he was stronger than her. He threw her against the wall and smirked

"No one here to save you. I am going to do whatever I want." He suddenly stopped as he was pulled away from her.

"You lay another finger on her and I will kill you. Do you hear me? She is not here for your enjoyment! Back off!"

She knew that voice. She opened her eyes to see Raynier standing there.

The guard scrambled to his feet. He was nowhere near the size of Raynier. He narrowed his eyes into a glare and left the cell. Akatila fell to her knees, but Raynier caught her and cradled her. He gently kissed the top of her head as she whimpered from fear. Tears formed in her eyes but not a single tear fell. He stroked her hair slowly, knowing it helped her sleep. She fell asleep moments after in his arms. He looked down at her and smiled gently before putting her down on the small bed in the cell. He fixed her hair and left quietly. He looked back only once and smiled before whispering something.

"They will not hurt you if I am here. I promise, Akatila. I love you," he said as he shut the door and exited to the main training area.

She smiled softly as she heard what he said but then drifted back to sleep. She woke up the next morning to hear voices in the cell with her. She opened her eyes quickly to see the guard and someone she did not know. By the colors and the way his kimono was she figured he was the master here. He grabbed her arm and put her in a different cell. It was a bit nicer than the previous one but it was not home. He smiled coldly at her before leaving her. She then noticed the young man in the cell. She knew who he was.

"What do you want?" She glared, asking him.

The young man said nothing as he approached her. She thought he was going to have his way with her, but he stopped just short of her. He swung, connecting to the right side of her jaw, knocking her to the ground. He put his foot on her side, pushing down hard but not hard enough to crack her ribs. She winced from the pain but tried to get free from him. She punched his leg, which only made him angrier. He grabbed her and pulled her from under him, slamming her against the wall. She suddenly recognized the young man. She knew better than to show fear to him as he was the general's son, Seto. No one was there this time to save her, she had to fight back. He punched her right in the face, causing her to black out. He smirked and dropped her, leaving her there covered in her blood.

When she finally came to, Raynier was sitting there beside her, tears rolling down his cheek hitting the ground. She moved her hand a bit to let him know she was awake. He looked at her, shocked she was even still alive.

"Akatila, I am so sorry. I should have been there for this, I could have stopped this," he said, clearly upset.

"Raynier, I am glad you were not here. You must let this happen sometimes or they will question you. I do not want anyone else getting hurt because of me. I am fine, I was taught to handle it," she smiled softly.

He sighed and nodded. He helped her up and hugged her gently before leaving the cell. She smiled watching him leave, refusing to show him how much pain she was truly in. Akatila did not know how long this would go on, so she knew she had to be smart when it came to fighting the general's son off. Raynier, though, went and found Seto. He punched him right in the face, causing the young man to shift. Seto shifted into his Bengal tiger while Raynier shifted into his dire wolf. Seto lunged at Raynier but was too slow. Raynier was able to counterattack and pin him down with his paw. He growled, giving a warning, but he became distracted as the master appeared.

"Attacking the general's son, are we now, Raynier?" the master asked, smirking.

"I was just seeing if he was on guard," he replied after shifting back to normal.

"I see. Well then, well done. Seto, you must always be on the ready," the master scolded him.

Both men bowed to the master before leaving the court. That was when the master decided to have a meeting with the entire camp. All the soldiers came running out of the houses, forming their lines thinking they were being sent out again. Raynier stood at the front, glancing every so often over toward the cell where Akatila was. He could see her watching and listening. The master waited a few moments for everyone to gather and the camp went silent. It was so quiet it sent chills down Akatila's spine. She was not sure what was going on but she knew it was not good.

"Our little guest, Akatila, will be staying with us for a while. No one is to go in and hurt her, do I make myself clear? She is now going to be a part of our wonderful little family. The first person I find out that hurts her will answer to me. Got it?" he spoke with a cold smile on his face.

"Yes, Master Goenjo!" the camp replied.

Her heart dropped. Not only was she now stuck in this camp, but the master is also Chezuv's and Malinter's father. She began to wonder if this was a setup, but she then shook her head as she knew better. *"If it were not for them, I would have died in that battle a long time ago. They would not do this to me. They will come for me sooner or later or I will break out,"* she thought to herself.

She slid down the wall as tears formed in her eyes. She did not know what to expect from the soldiers. Would they listen? How long would she be there? Her heart shattered, but she was glad it was her and not her sister. She sat against the wall as every terrible thought ran through her head until she heard footsteps coming from down the hall. She jumped to her feet and stood in the shadows of the cell. The person walking to her got closer and closer until the footsteps stopped. Her heartbeat so loudly she thought the person would hear it. The jail went silent. She slowed down her breathing to make less noise. It was so quiet she could hear the crickets outside the window.

"Akatila? Sweets?" the voice spoke softly.

"Raynier." Akatila sighed, stepping out.

"Akatila, I am so sorry for this. I promise I will do my best to keep you safe. I am not sure what their plan is, but I will find out. I think they are waiting for something to happen, or maybe waiting for someone. I am not sure. I will keep you updated as I find out more intel. Please try your best to stay safe if I am not around," he said, putting his hands on the bars.

She gave a slow nod knowing her time in the camp would be brutal. She just kept thinking about her sister and the others. Tears fell down her cheeks as she watched Raynier walk off. She placed her head in her hands and cried silently.

Akatila cried herself to sleep. In her sleep she dreamt of the others and how life was before this happened.

"Akatila! Wait up! Where do you think you are going?" Yukia asked, grabbing her hand gently.

"Oh, come now, Yukia. I am only going to see the ocean, you know that" she replied, taking her hand out of his.

"Sweets," he said, a bit sterner.

"Look, Yukia, if you are going to stand there and complain then go tell Master where I am, or Malinter. If not, then let us go already before the sunrises," she replied, running off into the shadows.

They ran through ShadowCry Forest together. They both shifted into their animal forms and ran even faster. Despite Akatila being a small-framed fox and Yukia being a large fox, she managed to keep up with him. She leaped over the tree branches that were sticking out of the ground, while Yukia slid under them, falling a bit behind her. She looked back at him, coming to a stop. She shifted back to herself and sat down on the cliff. The sea breeze felt wonderful as she took a deep breath and could smell the salt water. The breeze was colder, but it helped her relax. Yukia finally caught up to her and shifted, sitting beside her feeling the nice breeze as well. He put his arm around her as she placed her head on his shoulder.

"Akatila, promise me something?" he said nervously.

"What?" she replied, looking at him.

"That no matter what happens we will always be like this?" he said, not looking at her.

She gave a nod and put her head back on his shoulder, looking across the ocean seeing the sunrise. This is what they always did before a huge battle. She looked up at him and smiled. She started to say something but she felt someone shake her hard.

"Huh?" she said, snapping out of her dream.

"Good, you're awake! Now let us go," the voice spoke harshly.

Chapter Three

She woke up quickly, shaking her head as she was dragged out of the cell. She tripped over her feet trying to keep up with him as he had her by her arm, pulling her out of the cell. He stopped, allowing her to stand up straight and catch her breath. She looked around, seeing they had stopped in the middle of camp. He was talking to another solider before he noticed she was looking at them. The solider gave a nod and he returned to her.

"Lieutenant Colonel Seto, are you sure this is wise?" A solider approached, asking him cautiously.

"Are you really going to question me?" he replied coldly.

The solider took a step back, shaking his head no, Seto smirked, returning his focus back to Akatila. He slowly approached her. She watched his every move. Before she realized it; he was standing behind her. He placed his hands gently on her. It made her shiver before he wrapped his arms around her shoulders. He was so close behind her she could feel his breath on her neck.

"I know what you think I am, but you are wrong. One day I will show you, but for now you are just a prisoner and will be treated as such," he said almost sympathetically.

She gulped as he returned to being himself. He grabbed her arm and continued to drag her out of the camp. She did not dare to resist, kick, scream, or even attempt to fight back. She knew it would get her nowhere.

She tried to get a sense of where she was. She could barely see the sunlight, so she knew they were deep into ShadowCry Forest but she did not understand why. She could no longer hear the birds chirping, so she knew they had to be in a bad area. She looked around and the fog was so thick she could barely see Seto in front of her. She had lost any chance of escaping as she did not know this part of the forest.

Seto looked back and sighed softly. *"She can never know I am one of the good guys and that Yukia is the traitor. It would hurt her so badly. It hurts me to do this to her. I do not understand, though, why she does not remember me. I wonder if Yukia gave her something,"* he thought to himself.

He shook his head, snapping out of his thoughts, and sighed, seeing where they were. He knew she was afraid of him and it killed him, but he had no choice. He pulled her in front of him. She looked up at him and was confused. Akatila saw nothing but grief, sadness, and love in Seto's eyes. She looked away from him and she felt his grip loosen a bit. He shook his head softly and gripped her arm tight, making her look back up at him. He tossed her to the ground. She hit the ground hard as she felt the rocks dig into the palm of her hands. She snapped her head back looking at the general's son. It was only her and him, no one else, and she knew she had to fight back.

"So what do you want? Hm?" she snapped at him.

"Oh, Akatila, if you only knew. If you only knew the things I did, you would not be so hopeful about your precious little friends coming to get you," he smirked, looking down at her.

She got to her feet finally as she staggered a bit. He swung at her, but she was able to duck and avoid it. He laughed at her before grabbing his knife. She glared at him not sure what he was doing.

"A little early to be beating on the prisoner, don't you think? Or what? Does Master Goenjo even know about this?" she spat.

"I do not plan on that today, Akatila. I have other business for you. I know you have a secret, and once I can prove it, your little friend is dead."

Akatila flinched but glared at him.

The young man slapped Akatila across the face before kicking her in the ribs, leaving her there gasping for air. He stepped over her before kicking dirt onto her. He knelt, sitting above her slightly, and whispered to her, "He is not coming back. He is a traitor. And once I can prove it, Akatila, your little Raynier will be killed. Not to mention the traitor who ran, and you still do not know about that. How sad," he said, grabbing her, picking her back up.

He threw her back against a tree and sat down in front of her for a moment, gazing at her. He raised his hand to her but she did not flinch. He rolled his eyes. He could not figure her out and it drove him crazy.

Akatila watched him with hatred in her eyes. She knew if she tried to run, he would kill her and then kill Raynier. But who was the mystery guy? How did he know? She shook her head, realizing he was on his feet.

He grabbed her arm, pulling her to her feet as well. "Do not worry, I will not kill you yet. But the day is coming, Akatila, where you will be killed, and I can only hope I am there to see it happen. Such a prize like yourself should not be wasted, yet you would rather hide your little friends and protect them when one of them is a traitor to you. Such a waste," he said, dragging her back toward the camp.

Her head spun with confusion. *There is a traitor in the group. Who? For how long? Why? What could they possibly want? When did they turn their back on us?* These questions spun in her head and she did not even notice that they were back in camp and heading toward the cell she now called home. She was thrown back into her cell as the general's son watched her closely. She rolled her eyes at him and turned her back, facing the small window. She sat down looking out, watching the training sessions as she always did. She heard him leave and she wondered where Raynier was. He had not been by to see her in two days. She tried not to worry but she could not help it. She dozed off until she heard a familiar voice calling her.

"Akatila, wake up. I do not have much time," he said quickly.

"Raynier!" she said, running to him.

"Hey, sweets, I heard what the general's son did to you. Well, made you do, I should say. I am so sorry I was not here. We had someone escape last night and no one can find him. I think he was a friend of yours, but I am not sure. I must go back out and look for him. I will return tonight," he said, kissing her head before leaving the cell quickly.

She sat back against the wall wondering which of her old friends it could have been and why did they not come for her. She wondered if she had been forgotten. She wondered if maybe they were better off without her.

Meanwhile, Raynier knew who he was looking for as he left the camp with three other soldiers.

"Alright, listen, the man we are looking for is named Yukia. He is wanted alive. The master wants to speak with him. Alright, spread out!" he said to the men before parting ways.

He wondered why the master wanted Yukia. Why was Yukia even a part of any of this? How was he a part of this? Why did he not get Akatila out of the camp? Questions swirled in his mind as he did not understand or trust him. He did not trust him after he left Akatila on the battlefield. He shook his head and shifted into his wolf form and ran through ShadowCry Forest looking for him. He hoped he would be the one to find him, not one of the others.

He searched all night and could not find him. The other soldiers could not find him either, so they returned to camp. Raynier was nervous to see Akatila. He was not sure if he should tell her who it was, but more importantly, he hoped she was not hurt. He saw the general's son speaking to Master Goenjo, but Raynier returned to his bunk instead. *"In the morning, I will go see her and tell her what I know,"* he thought to himself before drifting off to sleep finally.

He tossed and turned, unable to fall asleep. He sat up in his bed and looked around the dark room. He groaned softly as he got out of bed and stood right outside the room. The night air was cold and whipped as if it was angry. He listened to the wind rustling in the trees. He looked up at the clear sky still wondering why Yukia did not even attempt to save Akatila. He ran his hand through his hair trying to figure out a reason. He paced back and forth before he saw someone in the shadows. He growled lowly in a warning tone as he shifted and went after the person. Raynier kept up with the shadow as he realized it was another animal. He wondered who it could be. He caught up to the animal as he shifted back to himself as the other animal had done the same.

"Greto!" he said, shocked.

"Hello, Raynier. I know you must have a lot of questions. Let me start with a few. Yes, I am alive. No, I was never killed. I was driven away from the girls that awful day. Yes, I have been working with Master Goenjo in hopes one day I could get enough on him for Chezuv. Yes, Chezuv knew I was alive. I asked him not to say anything. I heard Master Goenjo now has Akatila. I need to see her. Last time she saw me she thought I was a monster. Yukia is a traitor. He is the one who told Master Goenjo where the camp was. He is the one who wants to see Akatila dead. He was sent to gain her trust, maybe even get her to fall for him, and then he was supposed to kill her. I am not sure why he did not do it. But I need to go, I am supposed to be reporting to Master Goenjo in a few. I will find you again," he said rather quickly.

Before Raynier could say anything Greto was gone. He stood there so confused and shocked about what he was just told. He knew Yukia was bad but he never thought Yukia would ever try to hurt Akatila. He walked back to camp pondering the news. He lay back down and stared at the ceiling. He finally drifted to sleep after a while.

Meanwhile, Greto walked through the woods wondering if Akatila would even remember him. It had been years since that fire. He finally saw the entrance to the camp, and he pushed the thoughts to the side. The guards stood tall at the entrance to the camp. They knew someone was in the shadows, they just could not see who it was. Neither of the two guards moved as a man stepped forward. They both relaxed and stepped back into position. The young man nodded to them both and entered the camp. He looked around to see very few guards and even fewer soldiers. *"Well, then again, when you are the general no one would attack your camp, so why be on the guard,"* he thought to himself. He stuck to the shadows as he wandered around the camp silently. He stumbled across Akatila's cell. He looked at her and growled before returning to the center of camp.

Seto was now standing there awaiting the man. Seto narrowed his gaze spotting him before he finally stepped out of the shadows.

"Exactly what do you think you are doing here?! You know better than to show up here and creep around!" he snapped.

"Oh, I am sorry. For a moment I thought you were someone important." He shrugged, walking past Seto.

"Master Goenjo," he said, bowing his head in respect.

"Greto, it is nice to see you again. I am sure you already saw her. I told you nothing would happen to her as long as everyone did their part," Master Goenjo spoke calmly.

Greto stood there quietly as he zoned out as the master spoke. He nodded his head after the master was done speaking. Another man stepped out. Greto narrowed his eyes, shocked he was here. Yukia stood beside Master Goenjo as if he had done nothing wrong, as if he were waiting to be given praise. Both men stared at Greto with slight confusion until Yukia gave a cold smile and parted his mouth, beginning to speak.

"What is wrong, Greto? Surprised to see me? Surprised I would do this? Well, let me clue you in on a little secret of my own. While everyone thinks I am Shala's and Sprin's brother, I am in fact the master's own son. I chose Akatila as my mission to prove to him that I could do as he asked. I never cared for her, not like Raynier or Riku. I disappeared on the battlefield that day in hopes she would be killed, left for dead, if you would. However, noble Riku had to show up and ruin it. He is a traitor to us and needs to be taken care of."

His words hit Greto like a brick.

Greto bowed to Master Goenjo and took hit leave. He knew if he did not walk away, he would do something he would regret.

The next morning Akatila woke up confused as it was quiet in the camp. She could hear the crickets as the sun had not yet risen. She sighed, leaning against the bars, as she had hoped she would see Raynier. But she figured he was still out on the mission to find whoever ran away the night before. She began to wonder who the traitor could be. She then remembered how Riku had showed up randomly at the battle. *"No, it could not be him, he would never turn his back on me. Would he? Oh, who am I kidding? I have no idea,"* she thought to herself.

She looked up at the sky. She noticed how the colors blended from a beautiful orange into a soft pink. She shook her head trying to stop herself from thinking, then the cell doors opened. She glanced back to see Greto standing there. She looked at him confused as she had not recognized him. He remained silent as guilt filled his eyes and he looked down to the ground before speaking softly.

"Hello again, Akatila," he said kindly.

"Again? Who are you?" she asked, confused.

"You and your sister were so little when the fire happened. I am not too surprised you do not remember me," he said, looking up from the ground.

"The fire? That was an exceptionally long time ago. I do not remember much except getting told my father had died and my mother as well," she replied as tears filled her eyes. "Were you there? Did you see anything?" Akatila asked desperately.

"Yes, I was there. Yes, I saw things. But telling you would put not only you in danger but your sister and . . ." He stopped speaking.

"And who? Me, my sister, and who?" she demanded.

Greto did not speak another word as he shut the cell door behind him. He looked back at her between the bars. His heart felt like it was breaking all over again, but he knew she could not know yet who he was to her. He turned away and walked down the long, cold hallway, leaving the prison.

He turned the corner and crashed into Seto. He narrowed his eyes but said nothing. Seto just glared at him before walking away. Greto knew that time was running out for Akatila. He needed to figure out how to help her escape before it was too late. He looked around and wondered if there was a way to signal the others to say it was time. He saw some soldiers walking toward him and he decided now was not the best time. He backed into the shadows and waited for the time to be right.

Akatila remained silent as the night became colder. She shivered, looking out of the window. She thought about what she was told. *What did he mean Raynier is a traitor? Who escaped last night? How would I know them? Who was that man I just spoke to? How does he know me and my sister? Who else was he talking about? Does he know my father or mother? Maybe one of them made it out alive?* She wondered about it, but no one came to mind. She had hoped her friends would have come for her by now, yet she also understood that they could not.

She looked around to make sure the guards were nowhere near her. She turned her back to the door so she was facing the wall. She placed her hand out flat, her fingertips barely touching the wall. She smiled as her memories of her friends were projected onto the wall. She sighed as she watched her sister and Anoquv race back and forth by the stream when they were little. She then saw Yukia smiling as he stared at Akatila.

She heard footsteps and quickly pulled her hand away from the wall. She turned around to see Miko and her heart stopped. She could not believe who she was staring at. She had not seen him since the battle months ago. Her blood ran cold as she was face to face with the person who tried to kill her sister in the battle that should have never taken place. He gave a cold smirk that made her only worry about what he was about to do. He grabbed her quickly and dragged her out into the courtyard where everyone was waiting, including Raynier.

"Everyone quiet down! Today Akatila is going to fight for her freedom! If she can win in a fair fight against Miko, then she may leave us! If she cannot win, then she will remain with us," Master Goenjo called out loudly.

Miko grinned slowly, turning to face Akatila. Fear ran through her, but her facial expression was emotionless. She knew better. He ran at her and raised his hand as if he were getting ready to hit her. She was bracing for the hit when suddenly she defended herself.

CHAPTER FOUR

Akatila raised her hand in defense. She knew she should have let the young man hit her but she could not take it anymore. The young man gripped her arm, twisting it sideways, making her scream in pain. Raynier closed his eyes, clenching his fists. But he knew there was nothing he could do.

She continued to try and fight back as Master Goenjo watched from his seat. Greto turned, looking away as he could not bear to see it. Akatila finally snapped and went to shift but she felt a sharp pain in her side. When she looked down, she realized she had been stabbed. She looked back at the solider who was still holding the knife and she saw blood on the tip. She staggered, falling onto a rock. She tried to hold herself up.

"You said she would not get hurt! You said she would get a fair chance at freedom! This is not right!" Raynier snapped at Master Goenjo.

"This is fair. If she cannot fight now then she would be in danger out there, and better in here where she is safe. Now keep your mouth shut!" Master Goenjo replied with a sharp tone.

Akatila fell to the ground, placing her hands over the wound. Raynier finally could not take it anymore and went to jump over the wall to get to her but he was stopped by Greto. He watched as she continued to bleed, the soldier standing over her. Raynier and Greto both looked to Master Goenjo as he looked away, which meant to kill her. They both quickly looked back at Akatila, who was helpless at this point, and knew there was no way to get to her in time.

"No!" Raynier screamed at the soldier.

He distracted the soldier long enough for Akatila to scramble to her feet. She staggered a bit as she was dizzy from blood loss. She looked at

Raynier and he nodded to her. She turned and ran off as he shifted into his dire wolf form and caused a scene. Master Goenjo looked to Greto and glared at him. He looked down and nodded, shifting into his black bear form, and ran after Raynier.

Akatila got to the outside of the camp before turning around to see Raynier getting attacked by Greto. She winced in pain as she knew she could not help him. She felt a hand on her shoulder. When she turned and looked; she was relieved.

"You have to help him. He's the reason I was never touched in that camp. Please," she begged him.

He gave her a nod and whistled, calling the others over to him. She saw them, a red fox, an Indian leopard, a caracal, a Eurasian lynx, then the timber wolf that appeared out of the shadows, giving the nod to them all. They all leaped into the camp, getting the soldiers off Raynier.

She stood back watching, then Shala appeared.

"Akatila, let me see your wounds," she spoke as softly as she always had.

"I'm fine, really, just a flesh wound," she said, lying.

"And I am not blind either. I see your wound is bleeding badly. Now move your hand and let me see," she said with a bit more irritation.

Akatila nodded and moved her hands, but her gaze remained on the fighting in the camp. She could see everyone fighting and it only made her want to join. She began to fidget as Shala worked on her wounds. She saw the red fox get pinned and she whined, wanting to get to him. But she relaxed seeing the Eurasian lynx barrel into them, getting the red fox free again. That is when she saw Greto Ruv in his bear form heading straight for both the dire wolf and leopard.

She thought to herself, "*I have to get out there! I have to help!*" She shook the thoughts away quickly. She then noticed the bear was getting ready to charge. She shook free from Shala and ran toward the fight. She quickly shifted into her small-framed pampas fox and leaped onto the bear's shoulders. She dug her claws into his large, broad shoulders, which made him growl. He tried to shake her off, but she managed to remain clinging to him.

The red fox's ears perked up, hearing the growl. When he noticed the small pampas fox, he knew it was Akatila. He ran at the bear, but he was barreled into by another solider. Greto was finally able to grab onto the small fox and rip her off his shoulders. He had her by her leg, biting rather hard. She whined and yowled, kicking at him, trying to get him to let go of her. He tossed her to the side, sending her tumbling into the wall. She tried to get up, but his huge paw was now on her flank.

The timber wolf appeared from the shadows, looking right at the brown bear holding her down. He lunged at him, knocking him off. Akatila was able to get up, staggering. The wolf made her stay behind him as the bear continued to try to go after her. By this time Akatila's fur was covered in blood, a mix of hers and Greto's. She staggered, trying to remain behind the timber wolf. The wolf snapped at the bear's throat in a warning to back off, then Master Goenjo finally got out of his seat and yelled down to everyone.

"If there is to be a fight! It will not be in animal form!" he shouted with a cold smile on his face.

All the soldiers fighting shifted back to human form. Others were a little hesitant until Chezuv shifted from his timber wolf form back to being human. Akatila was next as her wounds were bad. She managed to shift from her pampas fox back to herself. Shala rushed to her side. Yukia shifted from his red fox and appeared beside Shala, while Riku remained in his Indian leopard form. Angelia decided to shift from her Eurasian lynx and sit beside her sister as Shala worked on her. The caracal remained next to Angelia, protecting her, and remained on guard in case something went wrong.

"We need to get her back to camp now. The things I need to help her, I do not have with me. I did not think there would be a fight like this," she said quickly to Angelia and Yukia.

"There is no way we can move her. We are surrounded, there is no way to get out. If you can fix her for the time being then I suggest you do so!" Ze appeared looking down at them.

Shala sighed and nodded to him. She began her work quickly as she knew she did not have much time to save her. Akatila, however, did not seem to pay any mind to the pain as her focus was locked on Chezuv with Greto. She was confused why Greto was doing this as he had protected her for most of the time she had been a prisoner there. Her eyes went wide when Master Goenjo finally stood up from his seat.

The soldiers backed up and remained in their lines, watching the soon-to-be fight. They remained on one side of the camp while Akatila and the others were on the opposite side. Ze shifted into his bear form and stood on the ready in case there were any unfair attacks as the dire wolf appeared beside him. The dire wolf glanced back at Akatila and let out a soft whine to get her attention as he flicked his ears, letting her know he was okay. She sighed with relief knowing he was okay. She looked back at the leopard who was still standing guard with the caracal.

Master Goenjo then let out a whistle and no one moved. He did it again and finally someone moved. It was the dire wolf, Raynier. Akatila's heart dropped as she was confused by what he was doing and then she understood and she tried to get to him. She ra to him but was tackled. Angelia and Shala were holding her down. They knew this is what Master Goenjo wanted.

"Raynier, I know you can hear me! Do not do this! Please! I need you. Do not hurt them; they will kill you! You are safe with us. Please come back!" Akatila cried out.

Raynier stopped for a moment. He looked back at Akatila, who was still being held down by Shala and Angelia. The sadness reflected in his eyes as he knew she would never understand why he was doing this for Master Goenjo. His heart broke. He saw the fear in her eyes despite the tears streaming down her face. He knew this was the only way to get them all out of the camp. Raynier took some paw steps forward before stopping again. He glanced to the timber wolf before giving a slight nod. Raynier then stood in front of the timber wolf, protecting him. Master Goenjo smirked.

"Raynier, you dare turn your back on me! That is fine. I suppose I should have seen this coming. You would protect her all the time from the soldiers doing what they wanted to her. You even killed for her. Does she know? Hm? Does she? Well, let us find out then." He spoke with such enjoyment that it sent a chill down everyone's spine.

"Akatila! I know you're injured, but you can still answer a question for me. Did you know that the young man who was trying to hurt you a long time ago happened to be Raynier? Remember? In the forest, you were attacked and savagely beaten. Only to find out who you were, and he killed his own father for giving him the order to try and kill you. He killed his own flesh and blood because he found out his father wanted you dead. Did you know that his father was once promised to your mother? Hm? And she got married to your father instead. Funny how rage can consume someone. And now, here we all are. Oh, and one more thing. Here is something to make you wonder and drive you crazy. Your father is not dead," Master Goenjo spoke loud and clear.

Akatila finally stopped moving as she heard what Master Goenjo said.

Her heart raced with confusion. She looked at Raynier as he was already looking at her. She turned away from him as she was now unsure what to think or how to feel. Raynier let out a whine, trying to get her attention, but the leopard growled, stepping in front of his view of her. Raynier looked at him knowing Riku would always protect her. He knew what had to be done. Raynier shifted back to himself and spoke with the coldest tone Akatila had ever heard her friend speak.

"Yes, I killed him, but he was not my father. You made me think he was. Did you not think I knew who she was? She is my best friend. She is the best thing in this world. And I will be damned if you hurt her again. You took her mother away, you sent her father away, you tried to break her and her sister up! But you did one thing right, Master. You gave me an advantage," Raynier spoke as he walked toward the soldiers.

Some of the soldiers gathered beside Raynier and shifted. Master Goenjo glared. Akatila could only watch as Raynier and a few soldiers ran at Master Goenjo and Greto. Yukia was now holding her down as she tried to break free and stop this as she feared Raynier was going to get killed. However, to her surprise, Chezuv shifted back to his wolf and grabbed onto Raynier's scruff, pulling him out of the camp. Everyone shifted except for Yukia and Akatila. They remained in human form as he carried her out of the camp. She passed out due to the pain finally consuming her.

Yukia kept a firm grip on her, but he was still gentle because he did not want to hurt her. He continued to run until they came to a little creek and he finally sat down, still holding her. He moved her hair behind her ear, which woke her up.

She blinked at him slightly confused about where they were until she saw everyone slowly appearing out of the shadows. She scanned everyone. Shala and Ze were the first to arrive. Her heart began to race. She spotted Anoquv, Harnuq, her sister, and Malinter, but there was still no sign of Chezuv, Riku, or Raynier.

"What do you think you are doing?" Chezuv spoke, looking to them both.

"How could you both be so selfish! What would Akatila have said or done if something happened to either of you!" he snapped.

Neither Riku nor Raynier said anything. They continued to look at the ground. Chezuv rolled his eyes as he walked away from them. They watched Chezuv walk off.

The silence that crept through the forest was eerie. No birds were chirping, no crickets, the only thing they could hear was each other's breathing and heartbeats. Raynier finally broke the silence with a sigh. Riku glanced at him in confusion.

"We can't let Akatila continue to think that we are the bad guys. Yes, we are assassins. Yes, we have these amazing powers and abilities. But what good are they if we cannot use them for any good! We can't even tell her the truth, Riku. It is killing me to think that she sees us as these evil people all while she praises Yukia!" Raynier shouted.

"I know the feeling, Raynier, but there is nothing we can do. It will all happen in due time. As for our powers, she does not even know about those. She knows we shift, but that is it. I would love to tell her the truth, I would. It kills me to lie to her. However, until we learn exactly why Yukia has betrayed us, why she is so desperately wanted by not only the general but also by Master Goenjo, it is safer if she doesn't know," Riku calmly replied.

"What if when the time comes, she turns on us for not telling her?" Raynier asked.

"I am not sure." Riku replied softly.

"She still does not even know that her father is around or that she has a brother Riku. What if she hates us after the truth comes out?" he said nervously.

Chezuv reappeared with his arms crossed as he glared at the two. He nodded to them. They both sighed, knowing it was time to face her. They followed suit behind Chezuv as they made their way back to the camp. *"I hope she will find out the truth soon,"* Riku thought to himself. *"She needs to know exactly what is going on before it is too late and she turns her back on all of us,"* Raynier thought to himself.

Chezuv cleared his throat making both men jump.

"You both do realize I can read your minds and know what you two are thinking about?" he said calmly. "Look, I get it. I do. I understand that she needs to know the truth. But Akatila knowing the truth right now is not what is best for her. It is not best for anyone in camp that they know. Yukia, for the time being, must not be revealed. I will be the one to let her know. She will take it better from me rather than one of you. Got it?" he said sternly.

"Okay," they both replied.

"Akatila, we know who you are looking for. They will be here soon, okay? For now, we need to get you fixed up," Shala said, sitting beside her and Yukia.

She gave a slight nod, her gaze still locked on the forest as she hoped they would show up soon. Shala began working on the wounds carefully. She gently applied each of the herbs until she stopped. She took a step back and pulled Ze and Angelia to the side. Shala's face was covered with concern, and fear consumed her gaze. Akatila had no idea why Shala stopped but she did not really care to ask as she was still looking for Raynier and Riku.

"Shala? What is wrong? Is my sister going to be okay now?" Angelia was the first one to speak.

"We have a slight problem. While the stab wound has healed, there is an issue. The weapon used to stab her was laced with some sort of poison," Shala said, glancing at Akatila.

"Okay? So how do we fix it? Is there anything we can do?" Ze said, looking to Angelia then back at Shala.

"I am not sure. I do not know which poison was used. The only thing we can do now is hope she fights it off or we figure out which poison and I can stop it. But right now, I am unsure how long she has," Shala said softly.

Angelia fell to her knees, crying. She could not control the emotions as she was furious, upset, and heartbroken. She knew she could not lose her sister again as she still blamed herself for sister being in that camp to begin with. Harnuq came over and sat with Angelia as she cried. He gently wrapped his arms around her. She placed her head against his chest and gripped his kimono as she tried to gain control.

Akatila saw her sister crying but was not sure why. She went to ask but then saw Riku, Chezuv, and Raynier standing in the shadows. She started to smile but she let out a scream of pure agony. Yukia looked down at her as she was still in his arms and became confused. For a slight moment Yukia gave a cold grin. He heard the footsteps and his smile faded. Everyone came running to her as they were unsure why she was screaming as if someone was killing her. Akatila lost all the color in her face as she began to vomit. Everyone jumped back as Yukia remained holding her.

"What is going on with her? Is she okay?" Riku asked finally.

"Riku, Chezuv, Raynier, she's been poisoned and we are not sure with what poison. She has to ride this out or if we can figure out what she was poisoned w—" She stopped as Raynier looked down.

"Raynier, do you know?" Ze asked him and saw the fear in his eyes.

The young man walked a distance as Akatila continued to squirm and scream in pain. Malinter, Ze and Chezuv followed him. Sprin decided to guard the entrance as he knew this did not concern him.

"Snake venom, it's dangerous to foxes. I think it could have been laced with that. Except it was not meant for her, the dosage was meant for Yukia. I heard some of the soldiers talking about it. Yukia is Master Goenjo's son . . . He is your brother," Raynier said, looking at Malinter and Chezuv.

Akatila passed out again as Riku went and sat with her. He looked around for Yukia, but he was gone. Rage filled him as he could not understand why Yukia would leave Akatila's side when she needed him the most. He gently played with her hair, keeping her asleep while everyone else went silent with this news. Malinter looked to Chezuv before looking back at Raynier. Both Chezuv and Malinter waited before they spoke. Harnuq and Angelia remained by Riku and Akatila. In case a fight broke out, they could move her quickly. The silence was finally broken when Chezuv spoke up.

"Does he know? Does Yukia know he is our brother?" Chezuv questioned him.

"Not that anyone knows of. He thinks his father is dead, which is why he was raised with Shala and Sprin. But there is more," Raynier said as the group walked away from Akatila.

He knew the danger of telling them everything, but they followed him.

"Okay? What else is there then?" they all asked at once.

Raynier sat down on the tree trunk that was sticking out of the ground as everyone else sat down close by. He took a deep breath and began telling them what he had found out. He looked in Akatila's direction and looked back down at the ground as he sighed, nodding to them.

"Alright. So I learned not only is Yukia your brother, but I found out Akatila's father is alive. Granted we heard Master Goenjo say that, but what he did not tell everyone was who her father was. Akatila has no idea who her father is because he supposedly died before she was born. That is not true. He is very much alive, and he has been protecting her since the day she was brought into the camp. Although I cannot say yet who her father is as I am not fully sure, I only have my suspiciousness, I can say if I am right, he will end up being a great ally. So back to other topics, I knew about the venom because, like I said, it was meant for Yukia. I know he is your brother and her best friend, but there is something off about him.

I am not sure why the dosage was meant for him, but it was. Akatila was never meant to be the one fighting. According to some of the guards, the person it was meant for had escaped last night but they figured he would be back," Raynier said quickly.

The group sat there in silence. They were still trying to process the information they were just told. Malinter had his hands balled into fists for so long his nails dug into his palms. Shala just sat there beside Ze in shock. No one had spoken, so Raynier groaned, shaking his head. He got to his feet quickly and threw his hands in the air. He paced back and forth for a moment or two before finally looking back at them.

"Was Yukia ever missing?" he asked cautiously.

"Not that we noticed. He went out and was gone for a few, but he never went missing for more than a day," Anoquv spoke up.

Raynier nodded as he tried to figure out exactly why that poison was meant for Yukia and not Akatila. He wondered how they knew he would be back. But before he could ask the question to the group, they heard Riku yelling at someone along with Angelia and Harnuq. They all ran back to the campsite and saw Greto standing there. Angelia and Harnuq were holding on to Akatila as she was screaming in pain again. Riku was screaming at Greto, getting ready to attack him, but Raynier and the others leaped in front of him, protecting Greto. They put two and two together and realized that Raynier was suspecting Greto was Akatila's father, so they knew they could not let him get hurt just in case he was right.

"Did you, do it?" Raynier asked, looking back at Greto.

He nodded and Raynier turned to look at Akatila and waited. Riku was still yelling at them to move out of his way, but Raynier's gaze and attention were locked onto Akatila, who finally stopped screaming and had gone silent. Riku heard the silence and turned to see what was going on. Akatila had woken up and was looking around slightly confused. Shala ran to her and checked the wound and saw the infection was gone, her fever had broken, and the poison was no longer there. She looked back at the others and smiled. They all relaxed and looked at Greto.

Akatila looked around, slightly confused why everyone was around her. At first she did not notice Greto. She noticed Yukia was no longer beside her. Riku was there instead, and everyone in camp was staring at her.

"What did you give her?" Chezuv asked calmly.

"The antidote, she needed it. She was running out of time. I would have been here sooner, but it was hard to track you guys down," Greto said calmly.

Riku looked between Greto and the others as he was still fuming about what had just happened. Akatila finally got to her feet slowly. Riku was the first to notice she was moving and ran beside her. She smiled weakly at him before Yukia appeared beside her as well. Riku glared at him wondering where he had gone. She let out a sigh of relief seeing everyone around her was okay, until she saw Greto. Her heart dropped as her eyes widened. The man stood there, the one responsible for everything. She narrowed her gaze as anger replaced the fear in her eyes. She tried to back up from him, but Shala grabbed hold of her before she tripped over a rock. Her body trembled as she felt her heart begin to race again. She noticed that Raynier was protecting him. She shook her head slowly as tears filled her eyes. She completely had the wrong idea.

Everyone took a step back knowing that she was confused, in pain still, and now furious. They knew better than to try and grab her. Raynier sighed, looking at her figuring she had the wrong idea. He took a step toward her, but she moved back further into Shala's arms.

"Akatila, it is not what you think. He saved you," Raynier said quickly.

"He attacked you! He attacked me! He hurt me and you are willing to defend him?" she screamed at him.

"Sweets . . .," Raynier said, looking at her.

"No, Raynier! He is a monster and should not be here!" she screeched.

"Sweets, just listen to me. It is not what you think. You have the wrong idea," he said calmly, but there was hurt in his voice.

"You're right, Raynier, I did have the wrong idea. To think you cared about me," she said in a whisper.

"Wh-what?" he stammered in shock.

"Yukia, get me out of here. I do not want to see Raynier," she said weakly.

Yukia smirked and nodded, gently grabbing her. Raynier took a step forward but Yukia was on the ready. He punched him right in the jaw, knocking him to the ground. Shala ran beside Raynier, as did everyone else. Chezuv narrowed his eyes and shifted, backing up into the shadows. Yukia continued to swing at Raynier. Akatila had walked ahead trying to get out of camp. She was unaware about the fight as she was lost in her thoughts. Yukia connected a few times to his jaw. Raynier knew better than to fight back as it would only hurt Akatila more. He allowed it to happen.

Shala knew that Yukia would hurt Raynier badly, so she began to prepare herbs as Angelia made a quick potion alongside her. Riku heard the commotion along with Sprin. Riku finally emerged from the shadows and barreled into Yukia, knocking him off Raynier. Riku swung at Yukia connecting to the left side of his jaw. Riku continued to swing but Yukia blocked most of the hits. Ze and Harnuq helped Raynier up. Anoquv quickly grabbed Riku off Yukia keeping him from killing him. Yukia smirked and slipped off into the shadows, going to look for Akatila.

Chezuv followed after Akatila quickly. As he had feared, his suspicions were correct. He noticed that there were four men sneaking about as if they were looking for someone. He recognized one of the men as the man who stabbed Akatila. He then knew he was right. Chezuv shifted into his wolf and began to hunt. He began taking them out one by one. He crept up behind them and used his paws to swipe at them knocking them down. He then would shift into himself and tie them up after he knocked each one out. He saved the attacker for last as he was closing in on Akatila. Chezuv remained in his human form and slid his arm around the guy's throat, slowly choking him and putting him to sleep. He tied them all up and continued after Akatila. Chezuv deiced to shift into his timber wolf and follow her. Akatila never saw the fight as she walked ahead. She turned back hearing paw steps, and she saw a timber wolf. She knew it was Chezuv. He shifted back to himself, stepping in front of her. His gaze was cold and dark. She looked down. She knew better than to argue with Chezuv. He was not as easily irritated as Malinter was. She knew to pick her fights. Chezuv sighed as he grabbed her arm softly and pulled her to the side. And yet she knew he was furious.

"Raynier was only trying to protect you. And you went and did that? How could you, Akatila? You know he loves you. He is getting beat up right now by Yukia, hence why you are by yourself. And do you know why?" Chezuv asked slowly.

"No," she replied simply.

"Because you were meant for them," he snapped at her.

He moved some brush revealing the men he had taken care of.

She looked up to him and saw that he had four guys tied up beside him. They had been savagely beaten. Her eyes widened as she noticed one of the men was the solider who stabbed her. He had a smirk on his face. Chezuv shook his head as Akatila stood there silent. She did not recognize the other two men, but she felt her heart begin to break.

"I am not sure why he would do this, but you cannot let on that you know. We need to figure out if maybe they have someone he loves or a family member they are holding hostage. We need to know why he is turning his back on us. That poison was not meant for you. It was meant for Yukia." Chezuv said calmly.

She looked at Chezuv. She shook her head, backing up. Chezuv quickly took the men away as he knew Yukia was coming. He nodded to her and disappeared into the shadows with the men. She felt hands on her waist and she jumped a bit. She glanced over her shoulder to see Yukia standing behind her. She forced herself to relax as she remembered what Chezuv had told her. She gave a weak smile as he smiled back at her.

"Come on, I want to take you somewhere," he said softly.

She nodded. She hoped Raynier was okay. She never meant for him to get hurt. She closed her eyes for a moment before she heard another voice and it was not Yukia's. She quickly opened her eyes to see Seto in front of her and she jumped back. But she felt Yukia's hands grip her arm tight. She looked back at him. He did not look down to her as she struggled to break free, but his grip only got stronger and tighter. She wished she had never left camp with him. She thought she could trust him, but she was wrong. *I want Raynier and Riku,* she thought to herself. Seto looked down at her and only smiled coldly. He nodded to Yukia as Yukia shoved her to Seto.

"You're a traitor! How could you? How could you do this to me?" Akatila cried out as the tears fell down her face.

"Very easily. Well, you were supposed to die on the field, but oh no, Riku had to be noble and save you. It is okay though, gave me more time to think of a way to get back at him. The day I came back, I saw that he really loved you, more than I ever did. But then again, my love was not real. I knew then that because Riku turned his back on his people that making him watch you get hurt would be much better than just killing him. He is going to know you got hurt, tortured, killed, all because of him. You see, Akatila, Riku was supposed to train as one of us. He did not want that life though, and Master Goenjo let him go because, well, he was Master Goenjo's favorite after all. But when he betrayed us, I became the favorite. I was sent to finish the mission he could not do. All I wanted was my father's love and attention. But no! Riku this and Riku that! And his obsession with you was unbearable! Nothing I did was enough! So, I came up with the idea of getting close to you. I came up with earning your trust. You were just a pawn. With you out of the picture my father would finally see I am better than you! Oh, that is right. You did not know that. Tell me how it feels to know that the person you love was supposed to kill you."

"You turned your back on me and the others because of jealousy?" she cried out.

"I will be the better person, and once my father realizes how pathetic you are. I will be the favorite. I will be the person he goes to for everything. I will take you out Akatila, trust me." He said coldly.

She just stared at him. She knew it was Yukia speaking to her but it did not act or sound like him. His eyes were the same, his voice was also, but when she looked at Yukia she did not know who this man was. Her best friend, the person she knew would never have done this. She looked back at Seto and was even more confused. Yukia smirked while looking at her before finally looking to Seto and clearing his throat.

"You should go. Master Goenjo will want her back. I will be at camp soon. I have to go explain all of this to the others so they do not come looking for her," Yukia said with a cold grin on his face.

"Well, you enjoy that. Come on, Akatila," Seto said softly.

He began taking her back towards the camp, however where he was supposed to turn left, he went right. She was so confused and lost in her thoughts she did not notice at first. However, she knew they should have been there by now. She glanced around snapping out of it. She noticed they were going the wrong way. She gulped but knew she had to say something.

"Seto, this is not the way back to the camp," she said nervously.

"That is because I am not taking you back to that camp, Akatila, I am taking you back home. Yukia does not know that I am in alliance with Chezuv, but Chezuv sent for me once he even thought that there was a traitor in the group. You see," he began, "I have always been on your side. Yes, did I hurt you? Of course I did, and there is nothing in the world that I can do to take it back. But I had to. I had to make it seem like I hated you. I never wanted to hurt you. Chezuv even told me I had to. They had to think I was one of them. But I would never hurt you," he said with regret.

Akatila walked beside him as he had already let go of her. She looked at the ground as he spoke. She took in every word. It all made sense. Whenever he struck her it was never hard enough to hurt. It hurt a bit but just enough so they knew he had done something to her. She then had an idea and she stopped walking. Seto looked back at her with slight confusion. She shook her head quickly; she had this quick memory pop into her head. She ran to the nearby tree; she placed her hand on the tree and it displayed the memory. Seto watched with amazement and confusion at what the memory was. Then he knew what it was, and guilt hit him.

"Oh, come on, Akatila, you're my little sister. I always will tease you. But I would never hurt you," a younger version of Seto declared.

"I will always protect you!" young Seto said proudly.

She removed her hand from the tree slowly in shock. Akatila looked over her shoulder to Seto, who was staring at the ground, shuffling his feet. She approached him before stopping just short of him. She tapped him softly. He looked at her.

"Is it true? Was that just a dream? Or was it a real memory?" she asked him.

"It happened. You were five years old; I was seven. I was teasing you and you tripped and fell. You were surprised how quickly I ran to you and helped you up. Dad and I bandaged your leg up and he sang to you as you fell asleep. I told you that right before you passed out in your bed," he said softly.

"I did not think you would remember that." He whispered.

She took a few steps back as she could not believe she had a brother and forgot about him. She wondered why she had forgotten him. She began to shake her head as her vison went blurry. Seto knew Yukia had to have given her something, anger rose in him. Seto quickly grabbed her arm, seeing something. She flinched quickly but she gave him her arm. He rolled her sleeve back a bit, revealing an odd marking. It looked like a burn mark, but there was roughness to it. He softly drug his fingers over the mark feeling the edges to it as if it was an imprint. When he looked closer, he realized it was Yukia's family crest.

"I cannot believe him! I knew there had to be a reason you did not remember me! I wonder if Angelia has the same mark," he said furiously.

She looked down at the mark. She'd never really paid much attention since she had had it since the fire many years ago. She shrugged it off as she noticed Seto begin walking again. She quickly ran after him, unsure where he was going.

"Where are we going?" she cautiously asked.

"Camp. Yukia is mine," he replied calmly.

She knew by the tone of his voice he was ready for a fight, as she had heard it a few times in the camp with other soldiers. Akatila remained silent the entire way back to camp. As they made their way back to camp memories flooded her mind. She could hear all the times her, Angelia and

Seto would play together. She kept smiling at the ground until she heard Seto stop. She looked up and saw familiar faces. Chezuv met them halfway. She saw her sister and ran to her. She embraced Angelia's hug as Angelia stared at Seto. Seto checked her right arm and Angelia also had the same mark. Chezuv knew then that this was the work of Yukia. All four of them returned to camp. Everyone, including Yukia, was standing there listening to his wild story about what happened.

"Seto and his men attacked us!" he began his lie.

"Where is she!" Riku demanded.

"I fought of Seto's men, but I could not get to Seto." Yukia tried to fake his sadness.

"I couldn't save her, Seto took her," he said, lying.

Riku stood there in shock on how something like this could have happened. Raynier had tears in his eyes as he felt this was his fault. Everyone was silent until they saw someone walking towards them.

"If Seto has me, how am I standing here?" Akatila shouted, making him jump.

"Yukia!" Chezuv and Seto both screamed

CHAPTER FIVE

"Yukia!" Chezuv and Seto both screamed.

The young man spun around to come face to face with Akatila. She punched him square in the nose, breaking it swiftly. He staggered back, instantly grabbing his face. He shook his head as blood dripped from his nose down his face. His gaze was locked on Akatila. His eyes narrowed as he could not believe she was there. Everyone slowly gathered around him as Seto stood beside her. Yukia scoffed as he got ready for the fight. Seto moved to step in but she grabbed his arm gently, shaking her head no. He knew this was her fight, so he sighed, stepping back beside Chezuv. Raynier and Riku did not move as they so knew what was in store for Yukia. Riku just smirked knowing what Akatila was capable of. Raynier was glad it was Yukia in the fight with Akatila and not himself.

"I am going to give you a chance, Yukia," she called out to him.

"And what chance is that? To run? To run and never look back?" he smirked.

"No, to explain to them why you turned your back on me! Explain to them why you would turn your back on them! I am sure they would be thrilled to know the real reason!" she snapped.

He went silent, his gaze was cold and dark. She could not believe the person she was looking at used to be her best friend, used to be a lover, used to be everything to her. It was as if she had no idea who this person was. She looked over to her sister, who had just arrived with Harnuq. Akatila glanced back at Seto and Greto but said nothing as she looked back, meeting Yukia's cold stare. She looked down at her hands realizing they were balled into tight fists. She smirked and snapped her head up, catching Yukia off guard.

"I gave you a chance. You do not want to tell them. Fine, but that does not mean you get to walk away," she said harshly.

Yukia could not even reach for his katana before she swung at him, no katana, just her fists. He ducked from her first swing but she was able to connect her right swing to his jawline, knocking him to the ground. She did not even realize she had busted her knuckles open, adrenaline kicked in as she stepped on his ankle to keep him from getting back up. He pulled a small knife out of his pocket and sliced her leg. She winced, staggering back in shock. Akatila looked down at her right leg seeing the blood trickle down her calf. She glared at Yukia, who had scrambled to his feet. She knew she could win against him if he did not shift into his fox. He flipped the knife around so he could fight better. She smirked at him, knowing he was not skilled with a small knife. She took a stance holding her hands up by her face. Akatila ran at him, but as he went to swing, she ducked under him. She slid on her leg under him, slicing the inside of his left leg. Yukia let out a scream of pain. He remembered she was used to fighting like this, he was not. Panic ran through him as he knew he had to get away somehow. He tried to attack first but she swung her right leg, her foot connected to the side of his face. She kicked him and knocked him to the ground, he laid there shocked.

"What is wrong, Yukia? Can't keep up?" she smirked.

"I can, I just do not cheat or fight dirty like you do!" he said harshly.

"I do not fight dirty! I just know my enemy's weakness!" she exclaimed furiously.

He lunged at her, toppling her over. He pinned her down. He took the knife and plunged it in her right shoulder. She screamed out in pain as still no one dared to move. They all knew this was her fight. She struggled under his weight. He had his legs wrapped with hers holding her down. She tried to kick him off her, but she could not get a good enough grip on him. He pushed the knife further into her shoulder, making her scream even louder.

Finally Riku could not take it any longer. Riku ripped him off her, sending him to the ground. He helped Akatila up, who was now covered in her own blood. She whimpered from the pain as Riku held her gently. Raynier stepped in front of them, protecting them both as Yukia got up. He glared at Raynier and Riku before drawing his katana. Raynier smirked and shifted instead. He adjusted his paws to make sure he was still protecting them. He glanced back, seeing Akatila still had the knife in her shoulder. He whined looking at her. She looked over her shoulder to him.

"Raynier, I will be okay. I promise," she said, trying to smile.

He knew she was in so much pain. He looked at Yukia, who had also shifted into his fox, but there was such a size difference between him and Yukia. Yukia ran at Raynier. He dug his claws into the ground to gain better traction and more speed, Raynier hunched his shoulders forward, ready to take the impact. Yukia leaped at him. He leaped onto his back, digging his claws into his shoulders. Yukia bit down on the back of Raynier's neck, causing him to growl.

Chezuv stood up knowing that despite the size difference between the two Yukia had better speed. He and Malinter both stood at the ready. They did not know what really to expect any more from Yukia.

Raynier could not shake him off, so he growled and charged at a tree. He threw himself down, smashing Yukia on the ground, causing him to let go. Yukia let out a yelp as he hit the ground. Raynier backed up a bit, growling. He let out a snarl before charging again, aiming at Yukia's neck. He got hit from the side. He tumbled against the ground. He shook his fur to see Greto standing there. He shook his head no. Raynier growled, turning his back. His tail lashed. He was furious, but he knew that Greto was protecting him and not Yukia. Shala had already begun working on her wounds. Raynier did not even notice his own wounds, his fury was in full gear.

"Enough!" Akatila cried out.

"Please, just stop, this is hurting her to see you get hurt," Angelia whispered under her breath.

Raynier looked over to Akatila, who was now sitting there by the tree with Shala staring at him. He finally noticed that his fur had patches of blood on it, and he sighed, shifting back to himself. He looked at Akatila, but she looked down.

Yukia shifted to himself. He glared coldly knowing that the fight was not over. He got the idea to attack someone else and finish off Akatila once and for all. He smirked before drawing his katana again. This time he charged at Angelia. He wanted a reaction from Akatila and he got one. Angelia's back was to Yukia. Harnuq saw him running and he tried to get to her in time. Akatila saw the same thing, but she was closer. She used up all her energy and shoved her sister out of the way. His katana hit Akatila's arm, slicing it open, but she was able to use what strength she had left to pin him and keep him there until Ze came over and grabbed him. Ze grabbed him quickly and slammed him against the tree pinning him. Shala and Seto both ran to Akatila. Angelia sat there horrified about what she just saw. That should have been her and not Akatila.

"Akatila, how about we get you cleaned up? I need to fix your other bandages as well. Can you go one day without getting hurt more than once?" Shala teased softly.

"Now, without me getting hurt, how are you supposed to be a great healer?" Akatila gave a light giggle.

"How am I supposed to be great if you're always hurt?" she replied.

"Hm, good point," Akatila chuckled.

While Shala was tending to Akatila, everyone else had gathered around the tree. Ze had tied Yukia's hands together and had him by the tree. Ze waited for Shala and Akatila to be gone.

She took Akatila into the tent while the guys handled Yukia.

Once they were in the tent everyone began to argue.

"If you hadn't kept the truth from her maybe this would not have happened!" Anoquv snapped.

"Oh really? Because telling her the truth would have been so much better!" Ze replied.

"Listen both of you, we did what we thought was best." Harnuq spoke calmly.

"I agree Harnuq. No one could have seen this coming." Sprin chimed in.

"What do we do with Yukia?" Seto asked.

"Kill him." Riku and Raynier both said.

"We can't kill him" Malinter stated.

"What else can we do?" Anoquv asked.

"We have to figure something out." Harnuq stated.

"Why can't we just kill him!" Raynier demanded.

"It is not what we do!" Malinter spat.

"And yet Akatila has been poisoned, beaten, kidnapped, stabbed twice. And yet this is supposed to be ok with me?" Riku snapped at Malinter.

"Enough, all of you. What's done is done." Chezuv spoke quickly.

Yukia took this time to begin to untie his bounds. No one noticed him doing this because they were so busy arguing among themselves. He was able to slip away into the shadows without being seen. Angelia who had been silent finally looked around and narrowed her eyes. She glared at everyone.

"How could you all be selfish? How could you all be so arrogant?" Angelia snapped.

"What are you talking about?" Sprin was the first to speak up.

"Who is missing?" she said, gritting her teeth.

They all looked around and never even noticed Yukia was gone. They looked back to Angelia with confusion. She groaned, rolling her eyes as she walked over to the tree where Yukia was being held. She stood there and still no one asked, just stood there in silence. She smacked her hand to her face, dragging her hand down her face in irritation.

"Oh, for the love of . . . Yukia!" she snapped.

"Wait, what?" Seto said, finally snapping out of it.

"He is gone! You guys were so wrapped up in arguing over what to do with him and who to blame you did not even notice he escaped!" Angelia cried out.

Everyone finally looked at each other with regret. They looked down before Chezuv finally spoke up. He waited until everyone stopped talking.

"Who's telling Akatila?" he asked.

"I will. She will not want to see any of you, trust me. You all messed up this time," Angelia said, turning her back to them all.

Angelia made her way to the tent. She took a deep breath and sighed. She knew this would not end well. She made her way into the tent, she saw her sister and gulped.

"Akatila, sis, I have bad news," she whispered.

Akatila looked up at her from where she was lying in bed. Shala looked over her shoulder with curiosity. She could see in her eyes that something was wrong. She sighed as she started preparing a calming tonic for Akatila, she figured it had to do with the yelling outside the den.

"Akatila, he's gone. Yukia, he escaped," Angelia said softly.

"He is what? How? When? Why?" she stammered.

"He just escaped, we do not know how. They are going to look for him," she assured her.

"We have to go after him!" Ze growled, speaking up finally.

"Ze, we all know that if we do, we would be leaving not only Akatila as a target but Shala as well. Raynier, Riku, Malinter, and I will go after him. Seto, Greto, Harnuq, Anoquv, Sprin, and Ze, you need to stay here and protect them," Chezuv said sternly.

They all nodded as Seto returned to his sisters along with Greto, Ze shifted and took watch on a nearby tree. Everyone else sat down around the fire. Chezuv and the others ran off into the forest to see if they could find his trail and bring him back to answer for what he had done.

Akatila began to panic thinking about how Yukia could come back. She felt her heart race with fear, and she began to tremble. Shala was glad she had made that tonic, she gave it Akatila. Angelia remained by her sister. Harnuq had entered the tent as well and sat with Angelia.

Akatila had fallen asleep finally due to the medicine Shala had given her. Angelia fell asleep in Harnuq's arms. Seto stood guard by the entrance.

"Chezuv, where could he have gone?" Malinter asked.

"I am not sure, Malinter. Riku, anything?" he called.

"Sorry, Chezuv, I have nothing. Raynier, what about you, got anything?" he asked.

"Sorry, I have lost it," he said, annoyed.

"Chezuv, we have lost the trail, he is gone," Malinter said coldly.

He nodded and stood there for a moment before turning to Raynier and Riku. He knew they wanted to get Yukia for what he had done to Akatila. He could see the hate burning in their eyes. He shook his head and turned to Malinter before giving a low growl.

"We are not alone," Chezuv muttered.

"Riku, Raynier, take the left. Malinter, take the right, and I will stay right here," Chezuv ordered.

They each nodded and did as they were told. Raynier and Riku saw a flash of something go past them. They both had a bad feeling about this.

Riku stopped in his tracks while Raynier went ahead. Riku looked to the sky to see the birds flying the other way. The wind had stopped and all was silent. He felt his body tense up. Raynier came back to Riku holding a small pouch of some kind. Both men looked at it knowing they knew this from somewhere, they just could not figure it out. They returned to Chezuv, who was waiting for them. Malinter had not returned yet.

Malinter shifted into his tiger form. In case of an ambush, he knew he could do more damage in this form. He stalked in the shadows when he saw something remarkably familiar. He stopped and gave a low growl as he backed up farther into the shadows. He returned to Chezuv with a piece of clothing.

Meanwhile, Riku and Raynier were looking at a piece of a katana. They looked at each confused. Riku turned away but something caught Raynier's attention.

"Malinter, is this . . .," Chezuv started to ask but Raynier screeched. *"Riku, move!"* Raynier yelled at him.

Before Riku could move he had been hit with an arrow in his left shoulder, he hit the ground screaming in agony, Raynier dove beside him as Chezuv and Malinter went after the attacker. Riku nodded to Raynier as he saw Raynier's hand around the end of the arrow. Raynier quickly removed the arrow in one piece. Raynier helped him up, and Riku shook the pain off as he knew he had to help with the attack. Raynier was grabbed by one of the attackers and dragged for a bit before Riku got to the attacker.

"How many are there?" Riku exclaimed.

"Right now, I am counting three," Raynier replied quickly.

The three attackers stood now in front of Riku and Raynier. Riku was still dealing with his shoulder, so there was not much he could do. The attackers ran at the two. Raynier dodged the first attacker but got hit by the second. The two men tumbled for a moment before Raynier was able to pin him. He still could not get to his katana, which was beside their campfire. He knew if Akatila saw it she would scold him for it. He shook the thought away as he saw Riku get pinned. Riku however, had had enough of it and shifted. Raynier saw the leopard leap into the attackers, who had now grown to eight in number. Raynier growled, shifting as well into his dire wolf. He charged at the attackers, trying to get to Riku. He saw a flash of gray on his left and a flash of stripes on his right and knew Malinter and Chezuv were back.

"Let's get out of here!" one of the attackers yelled.

The four of them watched the attackers run. They all shifted back to themselves and Riku revealed he had been injured. Chezuv tended to Riku as Raynier and Malinter stood watch. It was silent between them for a moment, until finally Raynier's curiosity could not handle it.

"Chezuv, why did they attack? Why did they retreat?" he asked, cautious of the answer.

"Yukia," Riku said softly.

"Huh?" Malinter and Chezuv said at once.

Before they could ask what Riku meant, he shoved Chezuv out of the way. Yukia was charging at them full speed in his fox form. Riku took the full force. He could feel Yukia's teeth sinking into his arm as he was being dragged by him. He felt every rock hit his body and it was torture. They both went tumbling when Chezuv knocked into them. Yukia finally let go of Riku, but the damage was done. Riku was covered in cuts, bruises, blood, he was barely breathing.

Raynier gently picked up Riku, who was now barely awake. Chezuv growled, standing in Yukia's way to Riku and Raynier. Malinter stood beside Raynier for support. There was a silence between them. The wind could be heard playing in the trees and the water crashing into the rocks from the waterfall a few miles away from them. Yukia shifted back to himself. Chezuv did the same. Malinter took Riku from Raynier as Raynier knew it was his turn. He growled, stepping from behind Chezuv, shifting to himself.

"What is your problem?" he spat at Yukia.

"Wait till your precious Akatila sees her favorite all beaten up, barely alive. Tell me, how will you tell her that you let him die?" Yukia smirked.

Yukia then ran at Raynier, katana drawn and at his ready. Raynier was much quicker and more skilled than Yukia was. Raynier ducked under his swing, colliding with Yukia's legs, sending him up and over Raynier. Yukia hit the ground with a loud thud. Yukia scrambled to his feet and did not move, just smirked as he put his katana away and leaned against the nearby tree. Raynier was not fooled, he remained at the ready. A flash of Akatila appeared in his head and he knew that they needed to get to her, so he withdrew his katana, placing it back in its holder on his side. He glared at Yukia, knowing he had something else planned. Chezuv threw a knife, hitting someone from behind Raynier. He spun around to see the young man falling to the ground. Chezuv and Malinter stepped up beside Raynier.

"You see, Miko and Master Goenjo want her, and I am not one to disappoint," he snickered.

"What do you mean they want her?" Riku coughed, speaking up finally.

"Wouldn't you like to know. But sorry, chum, I do not give up information. See ya." He grinned.

He vanished into the woods. Raynier tried to run after him but he was grabbed by Malinter. He shook his head at Raynier and let go of his arm. Raynier looked to Chezuv, who was staring past him. He followed his gaze to see another familiar face in the shadows. It was so faint that Raynier could barely make out who it was. When he knew who it was, Chezuv and Malinter had already shifted and run after the mystery person. Raynier turned to Riku, who was trying to get up, and helped.

"Hey, you need to rest. You are in no condition to be moving. How would I explain to Akatila that you died on my watch?" Raynier said, pushing him back down.

"Akatila does not care for me. Everyone knows you are her everything. And if she is happy that is all I care about," Riku said, gritting his teeth from the pain.

A noise from behind them made both men tense up. Raynier relaxed, seeing it was Chezuv and Malinter, but his eyes grew wide when he saw who else was with them. He knew that Akatila would not like this if they took him back with them. He wondered what Chezuv was planning. He could tell he was furious.

Chezuv knew they needed to go after Yukia, but they had Miko, and they would make him talk. Miko glared at them all. Riku was barely standing up. Even leaning against the tree, he groaned softly in pain. Raynier helped him sit down and applied new bandages to his wounds.

"Chezuv, we need Shala," Raynier said worriedly.

"I know. Once we get him to talk, we will get him to Shala and this one to a cell," Chezuv said quickly.

Chezuv and Malinter grabbed Miko and took him away from Raynier and Riku so they could get information from him. Malinter grabbed his knife while Chezuv pinned him to a large redwood tree. Malinter drove the knife into his shoulder so he would remain against the tree. Miko let out a scream of pain; he struggled to get free. Malinter said nothing as Chezuv stepped up first.

"Why do you want Akatila?" he asked plainly.

"I'm not telling you anything!" he spat, wincing from the pain.

Chezuv gave a cold smirk as he looked to Malinter and nodded. Chezuv waved his hand, turning away from them and leaving him with Malinter. Miko's eyes grew wide as he knew Malinter was very protective over Akatila. He knew that this man was also very heartless and ruthless. Malinter walked toward him very slowly as he shifted into his tiger form. He sat down in front of Miko watching him cry for help and wiggle, trying to escape. Malinter raised his claws toward Miko and he finally broke.

"Okay! Okay! I will tell you! Just get him away from me!" he screeched.

Chezuv stepped out from the shadows, nodding. Miko began to tell them that Master Goenjo wanted her for her abilities, and how he and Yukia had been in this all along. They want her so they can control how the war ends. Chezuv and Malinter remained silent as he spilled everything. Miko finally sighed, looking down from their gazes.

"That's everything I know. They want her alive for her powers, to win the war, and to create an empire based on fear of magic and shape-shifters," Miko said softly.

"Get him down, Malinter. We have to get back to camp now," Chezuv said quickly. "Get ready to go. Raynier, help Riku up. We are going back to camp. And we need to get there quickly," Chezuv said bluntly.

Chezuv took Miko from Malinter. Raynier helped Riku up and all five of them made their way back to camp.

Meanwhile, back in camp, Sprin had jumped onto the stump and waited a moment for everyone to gather around. Akatila looked around seeing everyone else had gathered for the meeting except Chezuv, Malinter, Raynier, and Riku. She sighed softly but she felt a hand on her shoulder. She looked back to see her sister.

"You know they both love you and want what is best for you, right?" Angelia spoke softly.

"Huh?" Akatila replied, confused.

"Oh, come on, sis. Riku and Raynier have been fighting over you for a while now. Sooner or later you will have to decide who really has your heart," she replied.

"Sorry, not all of us can have a Harnuq or Ze," Akatila replied sadly.

Shala heard Ze's name and she giggled, walking over to them. She sat beside them listening as they did not even notice Shala was there.

"I get that you are upset because I have Harnuq and Shala has Ze and they both take care of us, but you have to ask yourself who do you love," Angelia asked.

"She is right you know, those two fight over you constantly," Shala spoke up, making them both jump.

Akatila went silent as her face turned red. She looked at the ground as Ze walked over to them looking for Shala. She smiled at Angelia and Akatila before following Ze over to the meeting. Angelia then saw Harnuq and her eyes lit up. Akatila let out a small giggle at seeing her sister's reaction. Angelia smiled at her before walking over to him. Akatila let out a soft sigh. She watched everyone gather around the fire. She knew she had to be there but she just wanted to get away.

"Listen up!" Sprin called out.

Everyone stopped talking as they looked to him. Akatila could not see him as she was still on the ground so she could not see who else was there. She saw Malinter in the shadows with someone, but she could not make out who it was. She shrugged her shoulders and got to her feet slowly. Anoquv appeared beside her, helping her up. He gave her a smile and walked over to the others. Akatila turned her back for a moment and just listened to the forest. She listened to the birds softly chirping. The crickets had come out to play and the wind was making such beautiful music in the treetops.

"We found something out! We think we know the next move of Yukia!" Sprin called out.

Akatila snapped out of her daze. Anger built up inside of her. She knew better than to turn around. She had to calm herself down before she attempted to approach the meeting. She turned halfway around and noticed that Chezuv, Riku, Raynier, and Seto were all missing. Greto stepped up beside her, giving her a hug. She enjoyed the hug which helped her relax.

"Know that whatever happens we all love you," he whispered to her.

"What do you mean, Greto?" Akatila said, confused.

He looked at her with pain in his eyes as he retreated to Sprin's side at the meeting, which made her even more curious. *"Why isn't Chezuv running the meeting, or Malinter? What could be going on?"* she thought to herself. She noticed everyone had broken away from the fire, so she knew she still had some time before the real meeting began. She sat back on the ground before she got tackled by Sprin.

"Oof," she huffed.

"Where were you? Why weren't you at my meeting? Not as good as Chezuv's, huh?" he said, pinning her.

She giggled. "Nope! Not even close. Rather boring actually."

"How rude! I work hard on those, you know!" he said, getting off her.

"Well, next time do not be so boring and maybe I will pay more attention," she said, playfully smacking at him.

They both stopped, seeing birds fly overhead. That never meant anything good for them. Everyone got ready in case it was Yukia making another attack. But nothing happened.

"Hey, would you look at that? Chezuv is finally back. And so is Malinter, Seto, Riku, and Raynier. Think the meeting will begin now? Wait, they look like they have been fighting," Sprin said, concerned.

Akatila got off him and ran to get Shala. Ze was the first one out of the tent and to them. Chezuv had a few minor cuts and claw marks. Malinter was untouched, along with Seto. However, Raynier and Riku looked the worst. They were both covered in blood. Raynier was being held up by Seto, and Malinter had Raynier. Shala ran to them first as Chezuv disappeared again. Akatila could only stand by and watch. She wondered what had happened, perhaps they struggled with hunting. She heard a howl and knew it was time for the meeting. Maybe now she would find out what was going on and why they looked like they got attacked. She went to approach Riku, but he turned his back to her, not wanting her to see him like this. He knew she had no idea, but he could not face her.

CHAPTER SIX

As everyone gathered around the fire, Akatila noticed that something was off with Riku. She sighed but did not move. Raynier knew what she was feeling for Riku as he was feeling it for her; he just did not know if she felt it for him. He decided to walk over to her but Chezuv showed up, so he stopped.

Angelia was holding on to Harnuq gently. Akatila looked over to them and smiled. She was glad to know her sister had found someone. Her gaze quickly snapped to Chezuv as he had someone in his grip. It was Miko! She stared at him with confusion and hatred. She attempted to run to him; however, Malinter put his hand on her shoulder, keeping her in place.

"Listen to what he says first, Akatila. Do not let your emotions get the best of you. You are better than that," Malinter spoke softly.

Seto appeared beside Akatila. He gave her a soft smile before looking back to Miko. Miko stood beside Chezuv with a cold look on his face. His eyes were so dark they looked black. There was no remorse on his face or in his eyes. His grin was of pure evil, as if he had something planned. Akatila just knew, but she did not know what he had up his sleeve.

The camp went silent as Greto stepped forward and was the first to speak.

"Why is he here, Chezuv?" Greto asked cautiously.

"He is here as a guest for the time being. Until I can figure out what to do with him, he is not to be harmed," Chezuv said loudly.

Akatila could not contain it anymore and was the next to speak out. She felt Seto try and grab her, but she was small enough to be able to slip out of his grasp. She made her way toward Miko but she was stopped again, this time by Ze. Tears filled her eyes as she looked up at him and then to Shala, who appeared beside him.

"He doesn't deserve this. If I can show what he has done to me, maybe Chezuv will get rid of him," she pleaded.

"Akatila, we know what happened," Ze said calmly.

"WHAT?" she screeched.

She backed up shaking her head, staring at her friends. She bumped into Riku, who gently placed his hands on her hips, holding on to her. She glanced back at him. His gaze told her he knew also and was still going to protect Miko. She slapped his hands away. She was going to start screaming but Chezuv cleared his throat. She turned around and met his gaze. The fury that burned in her eyes only told him that he was correct.

"What is the problem, Akatila?" he asked calmly.

"The problem? Really, Chezuv? You are going to ask me that question after everything he has done to me? And you want the entire camp to protect him as if he was our own?!" Akatila growled.

"Akatila, you had better remember who you are speaking to. I understand you are upset, and you have every right to be. However, until we learn what he knows he cannot be hurt." He returned the aggressiveness.

She turned her back, only to be met by Miko's gaze. She wanted to hit him. She felt her fists ball up and her entire body trembled with rage. She glanced over her shoulder to see her sister and brother standing there. Angelia and Seto both looked at her with worry. This was not their sister, this was not who Akatila was. Ze would not look at her, nor would Shala or Anoquv. Harnuq shook his head at his friend before Sprin finally took a step forward. Sprin looked at her carefully before stepping back beside the others. Raynier and Riku both remained beside Malinter. She growled at all of them before looking back to Miko. He smirked at her. He knew she would not disobey Chezuv.

"Fine, you want to protect him. I'm gone," she said harshly.

Before anyone could speak, she shifted and shoved past Miko, running off into ShadowCry Forest. Angelia watched her sister run off. Tears fell down her cheek and hit Harnuq's arm. There was a moment of silence as no one could believe Akatila would think that they were protecting him or choosing him over her. Shala began to also fear over her wounds. Akatila was not fully recovered, she was going to be in pain soon.

Akatila continued to run. She thought about how everyone just stood there defending him instead of protecting or siding with her. She shook her head trying to get the images out of her mind, but it was too late. She did not realize where she was. She tumbled over the edge. She slid down the cliff, cutting all four of her legs. She bounced off a few boulders, hitting her shoulder and dislocating it. She yowled all the way down but no one could hear her. She got stuck for a moment. She knew better than to try and shift back to normal. She would be stuck in her fox form for a bit. She looked down at her leg. Her right back leg was wedged between a boulder and the cliff side. She looked down to see the river below her. She had never been this far from camp and did not recognize the river.

"Oh great, now what am I supposed to do?" she thought to herself.

She looked around to look for something that she could get her leg free with. She huffed when she noticed there was nothing. She wiggled, trying to get free. She noticed some of the dirt under the boulder was beginning to move. She growled from the pain but knew she had to get free.

Meanwhile, back at camp, Angelia began to pace back and forth as her sister had not come back yet. Everyone was starting to get nervous, until Riku let out a terrifying shriek and collapsed. Shala ran to him and began checking for any wounds, but she found nothing. Chezuv suspected it was the link between him and Akatila.

"Malinter! We need to find her now. She is hurt somewhere and Riku is now feeling the pain. If we cannot find her Riku will continue to suffer and so, will she," Chezuv spoke quickly.

"And what about—" Malinter was cut off by another scream.

Everyone quickly turned to look and saw Raynier was on the ground grabbing his right leg, screaming in pain. Shala ran to him but again found no signs of any wound of any sort. She looked over to Chezuv and shook her head no. He narrowed his eyes as he looked between the two screaming men and wondered how this was even possible, until he heard Miko snicker. He walked up to Miko along with Anoquv, who also heard the snicker. Chezuv quickly grabbed the young man by his throat and pinned him against the tree, his feet barely touched the ground.

"Now is a really good time to start talking!" Chezuv snapped.

"They will both die unless she is found. It is the poison I put in their drinks. All three are linked together until a cure is found. Courtesy of Master Goenjo!" Miko said, gasping for air.

Chezuv dropped him. Anoquv looked at Chezuv with worry as they still had no idea where to begin to look for her. Shala had given both Raynier and Riku some herbs to make the pain more bearable but they needed the cure. Shala placed her hand gently on Riku's forehead. She sighed and went to Raynier next. Ze came back with two cups of water for both as they were running a high fever. Angelia, Seto, and Harnuq had already left to go find Angelia.

"Malinter, you and Anoquv go the other way. I will check by the river. She normally does not go that far, but we must find her soon or we will lose all three of them. Angelia, Seto, and Harnuq went east and will also cover the west. You two will cover the south, I will go north. I am just hoping she did not go north. If she did, she may be in more danger," Chezuv told everyone.

"Shala and I will stay here in case Akatila shows up or the others get back without her. And to keep an eye on these two, make sure we can do whatever we can to help them," Ze said calmly.

Everyone nodded and went on their way. Shala looked up at Ze as she crouched down to Raynier and Riku. She shook her head as their fevers had not broken yet. Ze looked over at Miko, who was still knocked out from Chezuv choking him moments before.

Angelia, Seto, and Harnuq had gone all the way to the border of ShadowCry Forest going east. She looked at her brother and boyfriend with worry. Angelia was beginning to panic and fret that they would not find her sister in time. Harnuq let out a low growl as he knew someone was following them. Angelia and Harnuq both shifted. Seto could not but he knew who it was. Greto stepped out from the shadows.

"What are you doing here?" Angelia said suspiciously.

"You have not found her yet?" he replied.

"If we had found her she would be with us, instead of being lost, hurt, cold, hungry, and completely confused!" she cried out.

He said nothing else as he saw how it was affecting her. He thought to himself, *"What if she went home?"* He shifted into his bear form and ran off into the shadows. Angelia and Harnuq both became curious as Seto was already chasing after him. They ran behind him, following Greto. Greto knew they were following him; however, his only concern was finding Akatila before something bad happened. He ended up losing them in the shadows.

Meanwhile, Akatila was struggling to get her leg free. She cringed as it felt as if her leg was splitting into two. Her shoulder felt as if it was on fire, and she had no leverage to pop it back into place. She cried out in pain, knowing that it would not help her as no one knew where she was.

She whimpered from the pain until she heard a crack. She looked at the branch. It was finally giving. She did not even realize that if the branch broke she would continue down the cliff and hit the rapids below.

She wiggled until finally the branch broke, setting her free. Akatila tried to dig her claws into the cliff side but it was no use. She tumbled down the last part of the cliff side. She hit the rapids, which caused her entire body to sting. She was able to come up for air. She looked around and her heart sank. She saw the rapids getting bigger and stronger and knew things were about to get worse. Each time she tried to get the surface the strong current drug her below. She was losing the battle against the rapids. She got pulled under the rapid and into the current. She twisted and tumbled in the water. She did not know at this point which way was up. Without being able to get the surface her vison was becoming blurry, and she could feel herself giving up. Right before she blacked out from the lack of oxygen, she felt something pulling on her, but she couldn't see anything.

He dove into the water, grabbed onto her scruff. He growled in frustration as the current was strong tried to take them both down the river. He dug his claws into the ground and kicked off, launching them both out of the rapids. He landed on the beachy ground. He held her gently by the scruff. Her small-framed body dangled unconscious. He padded into the forest to the small camp he had set up. He shifted back to his human form. He set her down gently in the small cot. He sighed, looking at her leg. He grabbed the herbs he could remember. He made a quick remedy and applied it to her leg. Due to the pain, she was out cold. He was thankful that she could not feel the pain. He wrapped her leg up in some bandages and popped her shoulder back into place and let her rest. He sat outside the tent wondering why she had run this far. He wondered if maybe memories were coming back to her from her childhood that he thought she had lost. He shook his head and put the thought to the side as he heard a scream come from inside the tent. He jumped to his feet and ran inside.

"It burns!" she screamed.

"Easy, it is okay. Here, drink this," he said calmly.

Akatila could hear his voice. She knew his voice, but her head was killing her and she could not seem to focus. She blinked rapidly; however, her vison was not focusing. Her vision was so blurry, she could not make anything out, nor the person talking to her. She knew she could trust this person, so she did as she was told. She felt the cup against her lips and she drank what it was. The water had a funny taste to it, almost as if it was an herbal tea. She felt the pain ceasing and her head slowly stopped throbbing. Akatila let out a soft groan as she lay back down slowly. She dozed back off wondering about the man who was helping her.

A little while later, she slowly opened her eyes, blinking. She looked around, excited to be able to see. She noticed some things that were familiar to her. She tried to get to her feet but was still a little unstable. She accidently knocked over the teapot. It fell off the tray and shattered. She froze as she looked up from the broken teapot to see familiar eyes.

"Chezuv?" she said, unsure.

"Yes, Akatila, it is me. You can relax now," he said calmly.

She sighed, relaxing. She knew there had to have been a reason how easily she'd trusted the man helping her the night before. Now she knew why. She sat on the edge of the bed looking at him with slight confusion. He knew she had questions, so he decided to jump on it before she did.

"You are safe, and no, the others do not know where you are. Yes, your sister, brother, and Greto are worried sick. Yes, we took care of Miko. No, we did not choose him over you. We needed to know certain things that he knew. I will tell you everything you wish to know if you do not try to interrupt me. Deal?" Chezuv said, staring at her.

"Deal," she said quietly.

"Alright then. I will begin," he said as he sat beside her. "I will start with Miko since you think we betrayed you. We were able to catch Miko shortly after he and Yukia split. Yukia, we have not been able to find, so we grabbed Miko in hopes of learning why Master Goenjo wants you so badly and how Yukia is involved in this. We were about to send him to town to get put in a cell when you showed up. We learned that Master Goenjo wants you for your powers. Yes, I know about them. You have the ability to show someone the past as well as the future. He wants to use you to see how this war is going to end so he can plan and keep winning." He paused, seeing her facial expression.

"Um, well, moving forward. As for Greto and Seto, I think that in time you will come to realize that they had no choice. I have been working with Greto for an exceptionally long time trying to figure out how to get him out of Master Goenjo's grip. We almost had it until he saw you the first day in that camp. He came to me and told me he was not leaving because he had already lost you once and he would not leave you behind again, no matter what happened to him this time," Chezuv said, looking to the ground.

"Oh," Akatila whispered.

There was an awkward silence between them before a branch outside the tent cracked. Chezuv did not move but Akatila became nervous. She knew that Yukia was still out there. She grew even more nervous thinking it could be Master Goenjo himself. Chezuv saw her worry and got to his feet. He shifted into his timber wolf form and growled, staring at the entrance to the tent. Akatila knew she could not shift as her body was still too weak; however, she did manage to reach for her katana and was at the ready.

When no one came around the corner, Chezuv carefully stepped out of the tent, growling softly, looking around. He saw no one. He shifted back to himself and called back to Akatila.

"If you want to come outside you can Akatila, there is no one here but you and I." He said confidently.

"I am coming. I would like to know more about how Greto and Seto play into this. If that is okay with you, Chezuv," she said, hobbling out of the tent.

He nodded to her as he reached out for her hand. She smiled and grabbed it. He helped her gain better balance and sit down. She smiled at the warmth from the fire still going. She put her hands near the fire, rubbing them together. She noticed it was still dark out and looked to the starry night sky.

"First thing we should start with is the obvious. Greto is your father and Seto is your brother. Greto and your brother were never supposed to know you and Angelia made it out of that fire all those years ago. Seto was just a child, Greto had been roped into helping Master Goenjo. In exchange, you and your siblings would remain safe. One day Master Goenjo got word that Greto was helping us take him down. Instead of asking or attacking Greto or us, he went after you three. He knew the quickest way to get him to cave in to telling him everything was hurt his children and . . . wife." He said the last part softly.

"Wi-wife?" she stuttered.

"Yes, your mother was in that fire as well. You were little, Akatila. I am not surprised you do not remember her. You look much like her, appearance and attitude. Seto looks like Greto. It is extremely hard to deny that Seto is his son. As for Angelia, she is a mix between them. Greto knew that your mother and brother were outside that day, you and Angelia were inside. He tried to get to you all before Master Goenjo did, but he failed. He came to us for help. Ze, Malinter and I agreed to help. We all ran to the house.

By the time we got there we were too late. The house was gulfed in flames. Your mother was trying to get to you and your sister, Seto was fighting with some of the guards. Your mother was able to get Angelia out, but Greto ran in through the back to find you. In the time he grabbed you, we had gotten your sister to the woods with Shala, who was waiting. I went back to get your mother, but she had shifted already and was fighting the guards so Seto could get away," he said, pausing as he looked to her.

Akatila had tears streaming down her face, but she never made a noise. He knew this was a lot but she had a right to know the truth. He gave her a moment to take in everything he had just said to her. He got up and fixed some more herbal tea and got new bandages.

"However, later after we had gotten you and Angelia to safety, we learned the truth. Greto had been roped back into helping Master Goenjo, your mother was taken somewhere, and Seto was recruited into Master Goenjo's army." He said calmly.

Akatila stared at the ground in shock at what she was just told. She wondered about her mother. She wondered why Greto and Seto never came for her. She wondered why Seto did not tell her the truth.

"I can see you have questions, young one. Ask away, I will answer what I can," he said as he looked at her leg.

"Why didn't Seto tell me the truth while I was being held hostage? Why did he abuse me? Why didn't Greto come for me? Where is my mother now? Does Angelia know any of this?" she stammered.

"Seto could not tell you the truth. It was too dangerous for not only you but him as well. He never abused you. We created a figment, or for better terms a clone. Seto knew he could never hurt you, and if he did not do as he was told Master Goenjo would become suspicious and it could have caused trouble. As for your mother, we have no idea what happened to her. We are still trying to find information on her. Yes, Angelia was told all this information the morning you ran off, we just never got a chance to tell you," he said calmly as he changed out her bandages.

She sat there quietly for a moment as she watched him work on her leg. She winced as the new bandages were tightened. She looked to the sky wondering if her mother was still alive. She wondered what she was like. Akatila looked back down, meeting Chezuv's gaze. He handed her a small cup with some herbal tea. She sipped on it as she looked at him.

"You know everyone has a power, right?" he said slowly.

"Wait. Really?" she said, surprised.

"Yes. Everyone except a few have a power that they have gained full control over. If we go back to camp, perhaps everyone would be okay with showing you," he suggested.

She shrank back from that idea. She sighed, knowing she would have to face her family and friends at some point. She finished her tea and decided to try and buy some more time.

"Can we start going back in the morning?" she asked softly.

"You can't avoid this, but yes. I think traveling during the day would be better with your leg. Try and get some sleep," he said, standing up.

She nodded and tried to get up, but her leg felt like it was on fire again. She cringed from the pain but still forced herself to put pressure on it. Chezuv put his hand out to help her stabilize. She gladly took it as she was then able to put pressure on it. He helped her back to the tent. She slowly sat on the bed before he helped her put her leg up so she could relax.

"We leave at first light, Akatila. Try and get some rest. Tomorrow will be a long day," Chezuv said as he left the tent.

"Okay," she said as she fell asleep.

CHAPTER SEVEN

The sunlight warmed the tent slowly. Akatila knew it was time to get up and start the day. She winced as her bandages were soaked in blood. She knew she must have torn them open in her sleep. She placed both hands under her leg, slowly picking it up off the bed, turning and gently placing it on the ground. Akatila gently pushed her feet onto the ground. She knew today was the day she would face everyone. Excitement and regret filled her.

Chezuv pushed back the tent flap. Seeing she was up, he nodded and helped her out of the tent and sat her down by the fire.

"It is a long way back. We should get there, though, by nightfall if we can make good time. It will depend on your leg and how much you can handle," he said, changing her bandages for the last time.

"I will be fine. I just want to be back with everyone. I will suck it up and deal with it," she replied.

He nodded and helped her up. He let her lean on him as they made their way back to the camp. She staggered a bit, so he tightened his grip on her to keep her balanced. She sighed knowing she was a burden and it was her own fault. She knew it was wrong to run away from everyone. She still wished she knew why she had done it.

Chezuv could read her mind, so he decided to be the first to show her what he could do.

"I wish I knew why too, Akatila. I wish I could answer your question on why you ran. But that is something I guess we will never know," he replied as he helped her over a broken tree.

"Huh? Chezuv, I did not say anything," she said, confused, as she stepped over the tree trunks sticking out of the ground.

"Akatila, I can read minds," he said bluntly.

She looked at him as they continued to walk. There was a silence between them as she tried not to think about anything. He helped her over the stream as she finally wondered how close they were to the camp as it was now midday. She sighed softly.

"You can think, you know. I do not read minds all the time. I can turn it off and on. Trust me, I do not ever want to know what goes on in Riku's or Raynier's mind," he chuckled.

"That makes two of us. Chezuv, what if everyone rejects me? What if my power isn't as great as I think it is?" She began to worry.

Chezuv gently picked her up and carried her through the stream so her leg would not get wet and ruin her bandages. He sighed, gently placing her down. He stopped for a moment and looked at her with a gentle smile. He knew she was worried, he could see it in her eyes. He placed his hand softly on her shoulder as he knew she had lost track of where they were.

"Why don't you go and ask them? We are here. Akatila, understand that they will be mad, upset, excited to see you. Emotions will run high. They will ask questions, just do your best to answer them. Understand that everyone here loves you. You are our family, and with family comes fights. But it is about if you can make up or not. It's your choice," he stated before walking to the camp entrance.

Akatila gave a weak smile as she and Chezuv entered the camp. There was a moment of silence as there was no one in the camp that she could see. She sighed softly, looking at Chezuv. Her eyes filled with tears and sadness as she looked back at the ground. He nudged her. She looked back up to see everyone coming into the camp at a mad dash to her. She gulped and could not brace herself fast enough. Everyone but Seto, Angelia, and Greto crashed into her. They were all laughing and excited to see her. She smiled at everyone. They got off her and she slowly got to her feet as Shala began examining her leg. She looked around as she did not see Raynier or Riku.

"How could you?" Angelia spat furiously.

"We have looked everywhere for you! How could you be so selfish?" Seto growled with annoyance.

Greto said nothing, but Akatila could see in his eyes he was just as furious as Seto and Angelia were. Akatila did not dare speak until she knew her siblings were done screaming and yelling, and she knew they were not even close to being done. She looked at the ground as Angelia started back up again. Her heart broke knowing she caused this much pain.

"Seriously, Akatila, did you really think we would pick him over you? Was that it?" Angelia asked.

"No, of course not," she quickly replied.

"Then what? Because you cannot just keep running off like this! What if Chezuv had not found you? What then? What would we do without our sister?" Seto chimed in.

"I just got my daughter back, please do not make me lose her again," Greto finally spoke softly.

Akatila flinched from his words. She dropped to her knees and just cried. She really did not know she had caused that much pain in running away. She knew they loved her and would never choose Miko over her. She could not answer their questions as she really did not know why she got so mad and ran off like she did. She just ran. She sniffled as her siblings walked to her, giving her a hug. Akatila let herself enjoy the hug knowing she was okay and so was her family. She pulled back from the hug and yawned softly.

"Where is Raynier and Riku? Are they still mad at me?" Akatila asked softly.

"Well, not exactly." Sprin said stepping forward.

"Perhaps you had better come see for yourself." He added quickly.

She nodded. She limped following him as she could start to feel her leg bothering her. She got to Shala's tent and confusion filled her gaze. She looked at Sprin with a concerned look, he nodded to her. She slowly entered the den when she saw both lying on the beds. Her heart dropped. She had no idea what was going on. Shala entered the tent after her.

"Akatila sit down for a moment." Shala said nicely.

"Shala what happened!" she shrieked softly; she didn't want to wake them.

"Miko. He put a poison in their water before you left. Every time you got hurt so did, they. Except they got it a thousand times worse." Shala replied.

Her heart stopped; she could not believe this was happening. She then noticed what Shala was doing. She leaned over to see a tonic on the table.

"Shala? What is that?" she asked confused.

Shala let out a small giggle.

"It's a tonic, being able to have you here and see your wounds. I know how to help them. They will be better by morning. I am sure they will want to see you then." She said softly.

Akatila left the tent quietly and looked at everyone else. Her gaze lowered as she knew she had done so much damage, she had caused so much hurt. Chezuv knew she was upset so he cleared his throat getting everyone's attention.

"Maybe for the rest of the night we let everyone get some rest. It's been a long day for everyone," Chezuv finally spoke.

Shala heard Chezuv. She ran to Akatila for another quick second as she checked the wound to make sure it would be ok for the night. Everyone nodded in agreement and went to their tents. Akatila was the last to retreat to her tent as she looked up at the stars. She took a deep breath and realized that no matter what happened, they were her safe place; being with them was home. She looked at everyone's tents and smiled softly knowing that they were safe and so was she. Akatila got to her feet slowly and made her way to her tent. She was stopped by Shala.

"Yes, Shala?" she asked.

"In the morning, please come and see me so I can properly fix your leg," she smiled.

"Oh! Of course, Shala." She giggled.

Akatila lay down in her bed and dozed off listening to the rain come down lightly on the tents.

Angelia woke up the next morning to Sprin and Riku arguing outside. She groaned and got up. She rubbed her eyes, blinking, before seeing everyone was awake already accept Akatila. She giggled gently as she entered her sister's tent. She looked at how peacefully she was sleeping. She gently rubbed her arm, waking her up.

"Huh?" Akatila said, half asleep still.

"Get up, lazy! We have stuff to do today. Oh, and Shala said to come see her." She ended with a confused tone.

Akatila nodded, yawning as she tried to get up. She almost fell over, but Angelia caught her, giggling softly. She smiled at her sister before looking down at her leg, seeing the bandages were clear. For once she did not wake up with a bleeding leg. Angelia helped her change into something comfier and cleaner. They walked outside, and everyone was waiting for her. Shala glared as she approached Akatila. Shala usually was a calm person.

"Oh, you're in trouble," Angelia giggled, leaving her to Shala.

"Traitor," she muttered teasingly.

"What happened to coming to see me?" Shala demanded.

"I overslept, I am sorry," she said softly.

Shala huffed but gave a smile as she checked Akatila's bandages. Everyone had finally gathered around the fire and smiled at her. They were excited to begin the new training. Shala nodded to her, giving her permission to watch. Akatila sighed but was excited to see everyone's powers.

"Alright everyone!" Chezuv Hollard.

Everyone looked over and smiled curious on what was going on.

"We are doing something different today. Today we will be demonstrating our abilities or powers." He stated.

Everyone looked shocked for a moment then it turned to excitement.

"Who's first?" Chezuv called out.

"I will go first!" Angelia and Shala both said at the same time.

Shala and Angelia started working together. Akatila realized that Angelia was like Shala. She could make remedies and potions to help others, just like Shala could. She was smiling at her sister, being super proud of her, when she noticed Raynier, Sprin, and Anoquv step forward next. They all had huge smiles on their faces, which made her giggle at them.

"Ready?" Raynier said excitedly.

"For?" she replied.

Raynier smiled as he put a few jugs in front of her and started moving his hands in a circle. She looked at the jugs with confusion as she then looked back up to Raynier, she watched his hand motion carefully. Water from the jugs came floating out. He created a ring of water. Akatila stared at him with amazement. She then saw a ring of fire around the water. She noticed it was from Sprin. Meanwhile, Anoquv kept it controlled with a bubble of air around it. She exhaled just stunned by them. She started to feel like her powers would not keep up with everyone's.

Riku remained behind Akatila as he put his hands gently on the back of her head. He was able to project the ocean. She gasped as she saw the waves crash into the sandy shores, she could feel the warmth from the sun, she could smell the salty air, and just smiled. He removed his hands and it was gone. She looked back at him and looked surprised.

"I can make people see illusions." He cracked a small smile.

"Wow," she giggled.

She looked over to Ze, Greto, Seto, Harnuq, and Malinter; she was curious. She tilted her head a bit as she could have sworn Harnuq was just standing there. She looked around and saw him beside Angelia. She shook her head, confused, which made Angelia giggle. She blinked and he was back beside Ze. She raised an eyebrow in confusion.

"I have speed as my power," Harnuq stated grinning.

She started laughing. She shook her head in amusement.

"I won't use my power on you, Akatila. However, I will use it on Riku." Malinter grinned.

"Wait! Why me?" Riku complained.

Malinter grinned as he closed his eyes and focused on Riku. Akatila noticed how uncomfortable Riku looked, and she wondered why. Suddenly the entire area turned into a battlefield. She could see herself fighting with Yukia. She was confused. She could see Riku trying to get to her but Yukia killed her before he could get to her. Akatila gasped with not only fear but also confusion. She looked to Riku while Malinter ended the demonstration. He smirked, sitting back down. Chezuv smacked him upside the head.

"What was that?" she exclaimed.

"Malinter can project people's worst fear. Mine is watching you die and not being able to get to you," he muttered.

"I won't show mine, Akatila. Malinter's done enough damage, but I can control someone's mind," Ze said holding on to Shala.

Akatila sat there on the tree stump just blown away by everyone's powers. She knew that her power was great, but it did not stand a chance against theirs. She shrank back a bit before she felt Shala place a hand on her shoulder and nodded.

"Well, I have a power too," Akatila stammered.

"Come on, show us!" everyone chanted.

She nodded and closed her eyes. She had to think of a memory; she wanted one that everyone knew about. She thought about the time they spent the day by the beach. She put her hand out as if she were going to high five someone. She exhaled and the memory was projected. Everyone stared at her until they saw her memory. Everyone sat down and just watched as the memory flowed out of her.

"Come on, Ze, a little fun won't kill you!" Shala teased, running into the waves.

"Yeah, lighten up! Please just try and relax. It is the one time we can," Harnuq added in.

Akatila watched everyone and just giggled at them. She looked at

Ze and nudged him, and he finally cracked a small smile. He ran after Shala, diving into the water, splashing her. Akatila remained on the shore watching them. Raynier, Sprin, and Anoquv jumped off the cliffs and into the water, causing a huge wave and splash.

"Hey!" Akatila giggled from the shore.

"We are so terribly sorry!" they snickered teasingly.

Akatila rolled her eyes playfully and continued to watch them as Chezuv and Malinter showed up. Both looked at each other and ran straight for the water like children. Akatila sat there laughing at them. She had never seen them act like this before. Everyone seemed to be having such a wonderful time. She closed her eyes to soak it in.

Akatila lowered her hand as the memory faded. She looked exhausted from it, but she was smiling. Everyone stared at her in confusion at what had been shown and how that was even possible. They all turned and sat looking at her, hoping for an explanation on how she did that, on why that memory, and why she looked exhausted. She did not say anything at first as Shala was helping her catch her breath and help her relax a bit.

"I can project my memories. Any of them that I think about, I can project onto anything," Akatila said softly. "However, I can also do so much more. I can project what I wish will happen, the past, and sometimes the future," she said carefully.

There was a long period of silence as everyone took in what she had just told them. Chezuv cleared his throat, breaking the awkward silence, and made her giggle softly. She realized that neither Seto nor Greto had shown what they could do; she was curious as to why. She got up, but before she could Shala placed her hands around Akatila's leg. She looked down and Shala was whispering. She winced and flinched from a sharp pain in her leg. When she blinked and looked down again, she realized that Shala had used her powers and fixed her leg completely.

"Thank you, Shala." She bowed her head to her. "Hey, how come neither of you have said what you could do?" she asked her brother and father.

"That is because we do not have any powers. We are the only two in camp that have no powers, just our animals," Greto spoke first.

"Yep, been powerless all of my life. Guess I take after Dad," Seto chuckled.

Akatila gave a yawn, as did everyone else. They realized it was dark and they had been doing this all day. She gave a tired giggle as she became unbalanced. Riku grabbed her quickly and gently. He picked her up and she fell asleep in his arms. He took her to her tent, gently laid her down on the bed, pulled the covers over her, and left quietly. He went back to the others and sat down. They were all in shock still at what her powers were and they all wondered if that's why Master Goenjo wants her.

"To answer everyone's question, yes. Miko had spoken with us a few days ago and told Malinter and I that Master Goenjo and Yukia want Akatila for her powers. She can see glimpses of the future, which could tell them which way the war is going to go. She can show the past as well, so she could easily give up spies on both sides without meaning to. We cannot let him get her, at any cost. Akatila does not know this yet, but she is the key to this war. And now, both sides know it and both sides want her," he said sternly.

Everyone nodded and got up together. They stood at the fire thinking about how to help Akatila and keep her safe while still winning the war. They all yawned and retreated to bed, except Riku. He remained sitting outside of Akatila's tent in case she needed something or something went wrong. He knew that he was not going to lose her again.

CHAPTER EIGHT

Akatila woke up the next morning. She yawned and stretched before getting up. She shook her head, trying to fully wake up. She walked out of the tent to find Riku asleep on the ground beside her tent. She giggled gently as she crouched beside him and ruffled his hair lightly. He blinked, looking at her.

"Oh! You are awake! Good morning!" he stammered, scrambling to his feet.

"Did you sleep out here all night?" She giggled.

He blushed, nodding. Before he could say anything, everyone walked out of their tents, smiling at them. He looked at the ground as Akatila just giggled, walking to the others. She sat down beside the fire pit as Sprin began creating the fire. The morning had provided a heavy tone as the sky was still dark and it was cold. Angelia walked over to her sister, sitting beside her, shivering. Sprin finally got the fire to stay lit. He dropped to the ground beside the fire, enjoying the warmth. Chezuv was the last to step out to see everyone already awake. He chuckled softly, shaking his head to see everyone huddled around the fire, even Malinter.

"Alright, everyone, after everyone thaws out we have work to do," he reminded them.

"What are we doing again, Chezuv?" Angelia asked.

"Looking for a new home. We cannot keep living in a camp. We need a proper home to be able to continue our lives. This war has cost us so much as it is, we deserve to find happiness, love, a family," he said warmly.

Everyone smiled at the thought of having their own homes, working again, having families—except Akatila. She said nothing of it as she did not know if that life would suit her. She looked at the ground as everyone began talking about it. She could hear Shala and Ze talk about maybe having children after the war ended. She heard Anoquv talk about getting a wife one day.

"Can't you just see it? Me, opening up my own shop to help others get better and avoid getting sick?" Shala said with excitement.

"More importantly who would marry Anoquv?" Sprin teased.

Everyone laughed as he turned red. Anoquv shook his head and huffed. Sprin continued to laugh until Anoquv spoke.

"I'll find a wife the day you even find a girlfriend." He smirked.

Angelia and Akatila both sat there for a moment silent. They tried to picture either with a wife and they started giggling. Anoquv threw a tiny pebble at them both. Sprin just shrugged not saying a word.

"I don't know how I would react seeing Ze holding a child." Anoquv added changing the topic.

Everyone sat there trying to imagine Ze holding a child. They all burst out laughing. Even Chezuv let out a chuckle imagining that. Malinter approached Chezuv and huffed. Looking at the food stock area, they noticed they were running low. Chezuv placed his hand gently on his brother's shoulder and smiled.

"I will go this time. Enjoy some relaxing time with the others. I will be back in a while," he spoke quickly before leaving.

Chezuv decided to head toward town. Perhaps this time they would have some real food other than just meat. He came to a fork in the path. He became curious what was down the other path. He knew better as he had things to get from the market. Curiosity got the best of him as he turned to face the other path. He decided to find out. He went right instead of left. He followed the path all the way to this tiny abandoned, half burnt-down cottage. He approached the cottage slowly, he knew this place. He could not figure out why but continued towards it. Chezuv stopped when he noticed a small white rose on what would have been the mantle. He looked at it and then saw someone he thought he knew. The person's scent was all over it. His heart raced and his feet were running after this person before he even realized what he was doing. He noticed he was in town now. He looked for the person, but they were gone. Chezuv tried to understand how he got back into town. He wondered if the scent was here too. He sighed as he shook his head trying to gain his composure. He went and bought some food like he told Malinter he was going out to do. He could not get the person off his mind. He was dying to know if it was who he thought it was. He returned to camp.

Everyone was still talking, but Malinter and Akatila both noticed something was off as Chezuv put the food down and retreated to his tent. Akatila looked at Malinter with curiosity. They both shrugged and got up. They both ran after him. Malinter looked to his brother in confusion, but Akatila saw the look in his eyes; she knew he had seen something.

"Chezuv?" she said softly.

"Brother, are you okay?" Malinter asked, concerned.

"I saw her, or at least I think I saw her. I need time, I am sorry," he replied to them both before turning his back.

They sighed and took their leave, but Akatila was curious about who he meant. She looked to Malinter, who looked shocked. She nudged him and they went to his tent and sat down. Malinter was still in a state of shock but he shook his head, looking at Akatila, who was staring at him.

"You want to know, don't you?" he grunted.

"If that is okay. If not, I understand," she replied sweetly.

"Chezuv used to not be so emotionless," he began but everyone showed up.

He chuckled slightly as he led them to the fire. No one had any idea what was going on, but they wanted to find out. Everyone sat down, curious to know about Chezuv and the mystery person. Akatila sat on Riku's lap, Angelia was cuddled up beside Harnuq, Ze and Shala were sitting on the log, and everyone else was lying on the ground, ready for the story.

"Alright, so we were probably sixteen at the time. We were in the town square. It was just another normal day. Chezuv growing up was always causing trouble, always such a happy person and oddly cheerful. We bumped into this girl one day. Never seen her before, but I saw Chezuv and knew. She was probably fourteen, maybe fifteen. Her hair was long and jet-black, slightly curly. Her tanned skin made her big blue eyes pop even more. She was super sweet. They hit it off very quickly. I had never seen my brother act like that around anyone. He was romantic, lovey-dovey, and they were inseparable. They began dating and everyone knew that they were meant for each other. Everything seemed to be perfect for them. However, a few years later they were going to get married. Everything continued to seem perfect, until one day a stranger came into town causing havoc. He began causing trouble for some local shopkeepers. Then people started vanishing. Chezuv and I knew it was due to the stranger. But there was nothing we could do. Many people were taken, including her. When she was taken Chezuv was furious and heartbroken. He went to find the stranger, but they were all gone. Vanished without a trace. Chezuv searched for months but could not find her or any of the others. His heart shattered. From that day on he swore he would never love again; he would hardly show any emotions. And he kept his word. Our father was cruel and evil, would hit us, beat us. Chezuv never made a sound. He never flinched, never cried, never got angry. He remained emotionless," Malinter said calmly.

"Malinter, is that why he is in his tent now?" Sprin asked confused.

"Yes, Sprin, he swears he saw her. He thinks that after all this time she has come back and is here somewhere. The problem with that is I am not sure if he is telling the truth or not. I have not seen her or scented her in years." He shrugged.

"Malinter? What was her name?" Akatila asked curiously.

"Esmelina." He replied.

Sprin and Akatila both nodded. No one spoke as they were in thought. Akatila wondered about the girl, Esmelina. She wondered if maybe she had ever tried to escape. She also knew the horror of being a captive of war. Malinter sighed softly, looking at the stars, knowing his brother would never give up on her, as he should not. He hoped Esmelina was okay for his brother's sake.

Riku finally spoke out as his curiosity had finally gotten the best of him. "Malinter? Does anyone know who the stranger was?" he asked.

"We had our suspicions, but we never had any solid proof. It is as if the person just vanished after taking everyone," he replied.

Everyone went back to being silent as they all tried to think about who could be behind it. Perhaps it was Master Goenjo, but if that were true then they would have recognized him. Angelia wondered if it was a servant of the king. Despite it being a war, the King had yet to show his face. There had been rumors many years ago that the king needed new maids and servants. Who better than a single woman? Shala shook her head as she wondered if the person who took those people were still around. If the person was, then why? No one had noticed that Chezuv was awake and stirring in his tent. Malinter did not even notice this.

"Maybe the king?" Angelia asked.

"Maybe," Malinter agreed.

No one saw that Chezuv was standing outside of his tent listening to them and watching. He finally got fed up with it. Chezuv left his tent and approached everyone, which made everyone go silent. He looked around at them, his eyes were dark and emotionless. Akatila feared him.

"Well, now that everyone is done asking questions about my childhood and love life, maybe we could get some sleep?" he said, slightly annoyed.

"No," Ze spoke up.

Everyone looked at him, shocked. Ze was usually incredibly quiet unless spoken to. He hardly ever said anything against any of them. Akatila glanced at Shala hoping maybe she knew what was going on, but she shrugged her shoulders in confusion as well. Sprin stood up next, then Anoquv and Harnuq. They looked at Chezuv with frustration.

"We get it, you lost the love of your life. But that is no reasons to treat us like we are the enemy. We are your family, Chezuv," Anoquv said sternly.

"If the weather clears up, maybe we can go look around, see if what you saw was real," Harnuq suggested.

"Fine," Chezuv said softly, trying not to show excitement.

Everyone nodded and smiled. They had high hopes that come daybreak they would find something, even if it meant a small detail to let them know that she was there. That Esmelina was alive and that maybe she was trying to get back to Chezuv after all these years. Akatila smiled at the hope and everyone returned to their tents quickly. Akatila although did not return to her tent, she followed Riku. She lay down beside Riku and just smiled with excitement. He kissed her forehead and they both drifted to sleep.

The next morning was noticeably quiet. No one had gotten up early like they always did. The crickets, and birds were not singing like normal and there was a thick mist that clouded the camp. Akatila peeked out of the tent to try and see if anyone was awake, but it was silent. She went back and lay beside Riku. She noticed how cold it was. She shivered before lying down beside him.

Angelia also stirred and left her tent. She stood by the fire pit and looked around. She could not see a thing and began to wonder why it was so cold and foggy. She heard someone and growled, shifting. She noticed it was Sprin and she shifted back. She looked closer. He had blood dripping from his face and arm. He fell in front of her. She screamed and ran to him. Everyone came running out of their tents. Akatila saw the blood and saw Angelia. She ran to her sister thinking it was hers until she saw Sprin lying at her feet.

"Oh no," she whispered.

"Is Angelia—" Shala stopped talking as she got closer. "No, no," she stammered.

She dropped the bowl of herbs seeing her brother lying there. He looked lifeless. Chezuv ran to him and placed a hand on his neck, checking for a pulse. No one moved as Shala went into a panic. She cried, trying to get to him. Chezuv shook his head no. Shala screamed out in pain as her heart broke. Ze could only hold on to her, his eyes filled with tears as well. Ze gently pulled Shala back. Angelia and Akatila both cried looking at their friend. Riku, who had known Sprin for a much shorter time, was fazed as well. He knew Sprin had much to give and much to learn.

Shala finally broke free from Ze's grip and collapsed beside her brother's body. She pushed his hair back, seeing his eyes were closed. She looked at his wounds and she could tell that he had been ambushed. She quickly grabbed Akatila's hand. She jumped at Shala's quickness and fell to the ground at Shala's force.

"Use your power! Tell me who did this!" Shala cried.

Akatila stared at her friend's body in horror. She trembled as she went to touch his forehead, but his eyes shot open. Everyone jumped back in fear. He glared at Akatila and ran at her, screaming at her.

"You could have stopped this!" he screamed.

Akatila began screaming. Riku fell off the bed from surprise. She continued to scream. He tried to wake her up, but she kept trying to fight him. Angelia ran into the tent, followed by everyone else. Angelia ran beside her sister along with Seto. They both tried to wake her up, but it was no use. Akatila was in such a deep sleep that they could not wake her. Malinter finally entered and saw what was happening. Chezuv nodded quickly. Malinter placed his hand over her head and she became quiet. Riku laid with her back down on the bed and everyone quietly left the tent. He gently stroked her hair keeping her calm. Once he knew she was calm he left the tent and joined the others.

"Malinter, what was that? What just happened? Riku?" Angelia asked quickly.

"I am not sure. She was sleeping just fine. She started to mutter about Sprin and then she just started screaming," Riku replied, confused.

"About me?" Sprin said, shocked.

Akatila silently appeared outside of the tent nervously. Her body still trembled as she was not sure if she was awake or asleep still until she saw Sprin alive.

"I saw you die. You were ambushed. You said I could have stopped it," Akatila said from behind them nervously.

Everyone turned to look at her. Her body was still shaking badly. Shala ran and got some herbal tea to help her calm down. She sipped on the tea as she sat down beside Riku, who wrapped a blanket around her. Everyone was looking to her for more information.

"I am not sure what happened. It was cold and foggy. It was eerily quiet. No one had gotten up yet except Angelia. She had stepped out beside the fire pit. She heard someone approach and shifted, ready to attack. She saw it was Sprin and relaxed. As he got closer, she noticed he was covered in blood. He died at her feet. I went to project what happened and he woke up, screaming I could have stopped it. I could have saved him. And he attacked me," she stammered.

Chezuv nodded, knowing she was telling the truth, which made everyone look to the ground. Sprin was shocked as he could not look at Akatila. He wondered if she thought he was a monster. He closed his eyes tightly. When he opened his eyes, Akatila was standing in front of him. She looked up at him and then hugged him. Sprin was like another brother to her and Angelia. She knew he would never hurt her. He enjoyed the hug and relaxed as the sun began to rise.

"Well, no use in going back to sleep. Perhaps some training?" Sprin suggested.

Riku stood up, smirking at Akatila. He held his hand out, pulling her away from Sprin gently before he drew his katana.

"Training match?" he asked excitedly.

"With you? Of course," she giggled.

She drew her katana as everyone gathered around to watch the two. Akatila gave a slight nod letting him know to strike first. He ran at her but then stopped just as she went to trip him. He swung his katana, knocking her off balance. But he caught her, he did not want to let her fall, which she knew. She kissed his cheek, which caught him off guard. She gave a gentle elbow to his side, making him let her go. She staggered a bit to regain her footing. She snickered as he glared playfully at her. He narrowed his eyes, looking at her playfully. He took a quick stance. She ran at him, but he was quicker this time. He was able to dodge the attack, hit her gently on the back, and trip her, causing her to fall. He stood triumphant and chuckled, looking at her.

CHAPTER NINE

Akatila groaned as she got to her feet again. She shook the dirt off her and tried taking a stance again. Riku swung his katana at her, causing her to jump back. She exhaled, trying to regain herself. He smirked.

Malinter watched carefully as despite Chezuv being missing he still had to have everyone train and be ready and be the best they could be. Greto came over to Malinter and stood beside him watching his daughter lose in her training match. He looked to the other side and saw Angelia was winning her match.

"One is losing while the other is winning," he huffed.

Malinter glanced to the side and nodded in agreement with him. He then nudged Greto as he looked back at Akatila with Riku. Riku was staggering backward as Akatila had finally regained her balance as was fighting back. She was swinging her katana at him. Riku was stumbling backward trying to gain his footing. He was swinging his katana back in defense and was barely able to repel her attacks. He finally tripped over a rock, collapsing to the ground. She put her katana to the side of his cheek, the tip of the blade slightly pressed against him. He raised his hands in defeat. She smirked and then held her hand out, helping him up. She looked over her shoulder and saw everyone was standing there watching.

"Malinter I will return soon; I am going hunting." Greto said softly.

Malinter gave a short quick nod. Greto left quietly as they were still training, but Angelia saw him leave.

"Don't you have something better to do?" Akatila giggled to them.

"I was waiting for my turn. Unlike Riku, I will not go easy on you," Raynier said, stepping out from the shadow.

Akatila turned to face him. She narrowed her eyes playfully as she gave a slow nod and took a few steps back. Riku stepped beside everyone else and watched as he shook his head, dirt dropping from his hair. Angelia smirked and leaned against Harnuq softly.

"Ready to lose?" Raynier asked.

"Not today, not to you." She smirked.

He narrowed his eyes and drew his katana. He did not swing first but he charged at her. She placed her hand gently on the handle to her katana. Raynier had already drawn his katana. He was walking around her in circles. She still had not drawn her katana.

Akatila closed her eyes. She was listening to his footsteps as he still stepped rather heavily for an assassin. She smirked, knowing exactly where he would begin his attack, and she was correct. He lunged at her from behind, a little to the right. She ducked under him, sending him over her. He tucked and rolled, sliding a bit once he got to his feet. She grinned, finally drawing her katana as he ran at her again. Their katanas clashed before she began to fight back.

She knew that Raynier was taking out his frustration on the fight. She knew he knew she had chosen Riku. He knocked her back and used his elbow to crack her in the nose, causing it to bleed. She growled at him. She shook her head, glaring at him as she ignored the blood dripping down her face. Angelia and Seto both watched on, becoming concerned.

She snickered as she swung again, connecting this time with his back. She made sure she used the flat side of the katana so it would not cut him. He screamed in surprise before swinging again with his fist. She was able to duck this time and trip him. She knew his emotions were getting the best of him and this would be the time to shut down the training match. She watched him trip over her foot and tumbled to the ground. She chased after him and held the tip of her katana to his throat, pushing very lightly.

"Give up," she pleaded.

"You win," he snapped at her.

He got up off the ground and walked over to see Shala very quickly. As he was holding on to his left arm, she wondered if maybe she had hurt him. She felt bad and she could not look at him. Shala checked his arm and nodded to him, giving him some medicine to take for the pain, and bandaged it up.

Angelia glared at him as Riku stepped beside Akatila, looking at her face, which was still bleeding. Anger arose in Riku but he managed to hide it as he knew it was from training, but he wanted to know why he did it, as did Angelia.

"I still do not understand why he had to hit you in the face that hard," Angelia growled.

"Easy, sis, it was just training," Akatila replied.

"Yeah, but still! What is Father going to say when he comes back?" Angelia replied quickly.

Akatila had gone silent as she thought about the question. She really did not know what to tell her father. She was still unsure why he had done it in the first place. She assumed it was about Riku but she could never ask him that question. She was worried they would no longer be friends and she would lose him all over again.

Seto nudged her, snapping her out of her thoughts. He gave her a weak smile and she returned the smile. They both looked to Angelia, who finally caved and smiled. Riku, who was still not convinced, was standing against the post holding the tent up. Akatila slowly got up, a little lightheaded still, but managed to walk over to him. She stood in front of him. She stood up on her tiptoes and kissed his cheek gently. She smiled at him and finally he smiled at her. He chuckled at the fact she had to step up on her tiptoes to reach him. He looked at her and gently placed cupped the left side of face gently. He leaned down and gently kissed her lips. She smiled within the kiss before Angelia giggled.

"She has you wrapped around her finger. Good grief." She giggled.

"And you don't have me wrapped around your finger?" Harnuq chimed in from behind her.

"How are you feeling, sweets?" Harnuq asked calmly.

"I'm alright. I am more nervous for when my father gets back. Seto is still waiting for him and hopefully he can get to him before he sees my face. He will be so mad if he sees this."

Raynier was by his tent before he saw Greto enter the camp. Seto was beside him as he tried to explain what had happened. Greto had no idea what Seto was even talking about until he saw Raynier leave quickly. Chezuv had returned and approached Malinter. He knew there was an issue, but he decided not to ask. Chezuv stepped beside Malinter still curious but remained silent. Chezuv and Malinter watched the young man walk off and cooled down. They knew it was just emotions that got the best of him. Chezuv shook his head and rolled his eyes. Greto ignored most of what Seto said until he heard Akatila's name being mentioned. He ran to

Shala's tent; however, it was empty. He made his way to Akatila's tent and saw Harnuq, Angelia, Riku, Shala, and then finally saw Akatila. He saw her face, he saw the bruising on her eye and the bloody nose and the blood that was on her kimono as well. He glared, looking between them, and he continued looking at them and began to wonder who could have possibly done this to his daughter.

"Who did this?" he asked coldly.

"Father, please, it was just training and things got out of hand," Akatila replied, muttering.

"Out of hand? You call this out of hand!" Seto shouted from behind Greto.

"Why don't we just get some rest?" Anoquv spoke up, joining them.

"Yes, I agree. It is late," Shala said softly.

Everyone left the tent including Riku leaving just Akatila. She sighed looking down at her feet still pondering on what happened during training. She looked up to see someone standing in the entrance of her tent. Raynier approached and looked at Akatila with regret. She knew he meant no harm to her, and it was just emotions were running high between the two. She gave him a smile and he knew things would be okay between them. He nodded to her and walked off.

However, Chezuv did not think the same. He glared at Raynier before seeing something flash by. He straightened, sitting up, his eyes grew wide. He shook his head quickly. Akatila walked over to him looking at Chezuv with curiosity. She waved her hand in front of his face, gaining his attention from the shadow outside of camp.

"Chezuv, you good?" she asked curiously.

"What? Yes, I am fine. Go rest up," he said quickly.

She nodded slowly and walked away, leaving him and Malinter alone. The camp had gone silent since almost everyone had retreated to their tents for the night. Akatila looked over her shoulder to Chezuv knowing something was not quite right, but she also knew he would never say that. She sighed softly before entering her tent.

Malinter turned and looked at him curiously. He also knew something was up.

"You okay, Chezuv?" he asked bluntly.

"Oh yes, I am fine, just a bit distracted," he replied slowly. "Hey, Malinter, I'm going out for a quick errand. Watch over the camp while I am gone. I shouldn't be long," Chezuv said calmly.

"Alright but be careful. It is getting rather late," Malinter replied.

Chezuv left the camp as quietly as he always had. He made his way down the path heading toward town. ShadowCry Forest was oddly quiet. He came to the fork in the path. Left was the way to town; right was to an abandoned cottage. Chezuv turned right and made his way down the path. He noticed two men were following him. Their kimonos were the same, pure black with an outline of a dark red. He continued down the path despite knowing he was being followed. He came to the little cottage that was half burnt down. He looked back behind him to notice that the two men were no longer behind him. Chezuv was no fool. He entered the abandoned cottage and glared at the person standing there. He said nothing as the other person finally turned around.

"Chezuv, it's wonderful to see you again," she snickered.

"I wish I could say the same thing about you, Esmelina," he said hurtfully.

"Oh, come on, Chezuv. You still can't be cross with me? That was a long time ago. I had no choice but to leave you. I did not want you getting hurt or paying the price for something I had done," she said, looking at him.

Chezuv did not meet her gaze. She sighed and sat down at the little table in the middle of the room. He remained by the door. The two men appeared behind Esmelina. She looked at Chezuv with hurt and regret in her eyes. She sniffled as tears began to fall down her cheeks. Chezuv finally looked closer at her. The Esmelina he knew and loved so dearly was not the same person he was staring at. Her brown hair was now black, her gentle blue eyes were full of regret, her cheeks were not rosy like they always were, and there was something off about the way she spoke. He suddenly knew it was not Esmelina that he was looking at.

"Where is she?" Chezuv growled coldly.

"Oh darn, you finally figured out it was not your precious lover. Shucks, I thought I played her very well," Nakamyomi snickered, standing up.

Nakamyomi snapped her fingers and five guys jumped from behind Chezuv, knocking him to the ground. They kicked and hit him until they knocked him out. They dragged him a few miles north to a small camp, where she had him tied up to a wooden post in a cell. The men continued to beat Chezuv until she entered the cell.

Chezuv looked at her but could barely focus on her. His eyes were swollen and he was covered in blood. He coughed and spit up some blood as he glared at her.

"So now are you going to tell me what I want to know? Or can I just kill you?" she asked.

"Depends, what do you want to know? If it is how to find a heart and some beauty tips, I am not the guy you're looking for." He snickered before coughing again.

She backhanded him, causing him to wince again from the pain. He looked back at her and smirked before spitting some blood on her face and then chuckled weakly. She growled, wiping the blood away and nodding to the guard, who hit Chezuv so hard it dislocated his right shoulder. He finally yelled out from the pain.

"Oh, that is right, you do not know! Oh, here, let me lift your spirits some." Nakamyomi laughed.

A guard brought in another prisoner. She was covered in bruises and cut marks. Her hair was down but Chezuv knew that scent, he knew the prisoner. He whined softly as the person looked up slightly. Despite hardly being able to see, he knew it was Esmelina. He could see her beautiful blue eyes forming with tears.

"Chezuv!" she cried out, trying to get to him.

"Esmelina?" he coughed.

She struggled to get to him but the guard held her tightly. She looked at him completely beaten and destroyed. She knew he could last a long time but she could not stand to see him like this. He looked away from her as she looked at the ground. The guard took her back to her cell. Nakamyomi stood in front of Chezuv grinning ear to ear.

"Now how about a deal?" she suggested calmly.

"What?" he winced?

"Information for the freedom of Esmelina. She's been a prisoner of mine for many years. I am sure you want her to be safe," she said, playing with his emotions.

"Despite my love for her, I will not tell you what you want to know," he grimaced.

"Chezuv, you do not know what I want yet," she said, confused.

He chuckled and then groaned from the pain. She growled, leaving him alone. He thought about how he'd been told Esmelina was dead and that he would never see her again. He knew he had to get out but he also knew he could not take her; he did not have that kind of strength. He passed out from the pain. He knew come the following day he had to break out and get back to the others. He dreamt of seeing his friends and brother again, he dreamt of having a family with the love of his life. His dream was short-lived as he woke up to cold water being thrown at him. He gasped awake and shivered from the cold. He glared at Nakamyomi. She chuckled, leaving him again.

"Okay, this is my chance," he said to himself.

He looked at his hands knowing this would hurt. He looked at the rope and began to chew through it. The water from the ropes rubbed against his hands, causing them to bleed. He knew he had to break free. After a little while of trying he finally got through and the ropes snapped. He fell to the ground. He struggled to get up. He staggered out of the cell. He saw some guards coming his way and he ducked behind a wall. When he saw it was Emelina's cell, he ran to her, but she was so badly hurt. He gently pushed her hair back. She flinched until she noticed who it was and she whimpered softly.

"I will come back for you," he promised.

She nodded. He kissed her lips softly. It broke his heart to have finally found her and then having to leave her behind. He was not sure if she would still be here when he came back for her, but he would not let her go again. He ducked out of the cell when he heard the guards yelling that he had escaped.

Nakamyomi came running, passing him without even knowing it. He got outside of the small camp and shifted. He began to run but he barely had any strength. He knew it would be a long way back to his camp and there would be hell to pay from his friends and family.

"Has anyone seen Chezuv?" Malinter asked.

"Now that you mention it, I have not seen him since day before yesterday. He has not returned?" Ze said, confused.

"No! And he is never like this! We need to go find him!" Malinter declared.

"Malinter, it is dark. There is no way we will be able to find him," Ze snapped.

"I do not care. I will go look myself!" Malinter growled.

Chezuv ran through ShadowCry Forest staggering. He had two soldiers running after him but someone saved him again. He saw a glimpse of white tiger. He knew who it was but was confused about how. He kept running until he got to the camp. He shifted and could hear everyone arguing.

"Malinter! Be reasonable! You will not be able to find him tonight! Wait until the morning. We will separate into teams and find him," Ze snapped.

"I do not care if it is dark or not! I must find him! My brother has never been gone for two days!" Malinter challenged.

"Both of you stop it!" Akatila pleaded.

CHAPTER TEN

Malinter narrowed his eyes and readied his sword as the figure continued to approach them. Harnuq pushed Angelia slightly behind him as Riku stepped slightly in front of Akatila. The figure stopped just short of them being able to see who it was. Malinter growled as he shifted, getting ready to attack. Akatila glanced around Riku. She was able to make out more than the others. She knew who it was and her eyes grew wide. She shoved past Riku and jumped in front of everyone.

"Wait!" she screamed out.

Everyone looked at her confused about why she would be protecting this person. Malinter then knew who it was. The wind had changed direction. They were downwind, she could not smell the person. However, the winds changed direction so they were now upwind. He caught the person's scent. He shifted back to himself, which made everyone very curious as to who this person was. Akatila sighed with relief as she turned to face the person. The person finally stepped out of the shadows, revealing himself.

"Chezuv!" everyone said, shocked.

He was covered in dried blood. As he fell, Akatila tried to catch him but his weight was too much for her. They both fell, him landing on top of her. Malinter ran over and picked him up while Angelia helped Akatila back up. They all looked at Chezuv with fury and anguish to see him in such a state. Shala came running out with some herbs and remedies. Malinter and Ze both grabbed Chezuv and took him back to Shala's tent. They paced him gently on the bed while Shala came in. She sighed, looking at her friend. She looked to Ze and Malinter.

"I will need fresh water. I will examine him. You both can wait outside," she said softly.

"I will go get some fresh water," Ze said quickly as he left.

"Shala, what could have done this? Who could have done this?" Malinter said softly.

Shala was taken back at how Malinter's voice was exceptionally soft, and she could see the hurt in his eyes. She sighed, shaking her head. She knew she did not have the answers but she could help him. Malinter took his leave so she could work.

Malinter sat outside the tent. He crossed his legs and tried to calm down as he only wanted to know his brother would be okay and where he could find the person or people responsible for this.

Ze ran down with two jugs to the riverside. He carefully placed the jugs in the water and let each one fill up. He knew that Shala would need as much water as possible to clean his wounds and to clean him up.

Meanwhile, back at camp, everyone looked around but never said a word. Everyone was on edge as they were shocked. Chezuv had been missing for two days and no one knew what happened or where he had gone. Angelia and Harnuq sat on the ground beside the fire. Raynier was standing with Greto and Seto. Akatila sat with Riku before Shala stepped out. Everyone jumped to their feet in hopes she was able to save him. She gave Malinter a small smile and nodded to everyone. They all sighed softly.

"When can I see him?" Malinter asked quickly.

"He is asleep for now but you may sit with him until he wakes up if you like," she said gently.

He nodded to her and quietly entered the tent. He sat beside his brother, looking at him. He looked much better as there was no longer any dried blood on his clothes or on his skin. Malinter looked over the bruising Chezuv had. He had never seen his brother in such a bad condition before. He sighed, placing his head in his hands.

"Akatila," Shala said quietly.

"Yes, Shala?" she replied, curious.

"You can help. You can project his memory so we can see what happened and who did it," she said gently.

Akatila did not hesitate. She quickly nodded, agreeing. They both entered the tent, where Malinter was still sitting beside Chezuv, who was still fast asleep. Malinter at first did not stir as he had not heard them yet. Akatila let out a small whine to get his attention. He snapped his head up, his eyes were red from crying and not sleeping at all. Shala sighed softly.

"Malinter, we have come up with a solution," Shala said softly.

"Let us go outside and talk about this," Malinter whispered.

"What is going on, Shala? What are you talking about a plan?" he asked cautiously.

Everyone else gathered around as they were hoping they could come up with a plan on how they can help Chezuv—what happened, where it happened, and who was the cause of it. They all walked over to the fire and everyone took a seat except for Shala and Akatila; they remained standing.

"The best way to help Chezuv is to know what happened, correct?" Akatila asked.

"Yes, of course, but with him still unconscious we can't figure it out," Malinter replied.

"I can show you what happened. If I put my hand over his forehead, I should be able to project his latest memory even with him asleep. He will never know, and then we can figure out what happened and who caused it," Akatila stated quickly.

Malinter did not like the idea of doing this without his brother knowing; however, they needed to know what happened. He sighed softly and nodded as they approached the group. Shala looked nervous, but she knew this would work, it had to. Everyone had already heard the plan and they all nodded, agreeing. Greto smiled confidently at Akatila as she went into the tent.

She sat beside Chezuv, worried. He looked terrible, and she felt awful that this had happened to him. She gently placed her hand on his forehead and looked at him.

"Alright, Chezuv, let us find out what happened and who caused it, shall we?" she whispered.

She was able to project the last memory he had. She was shocked at who she saw in the memory. She quickly pulled her hand back and ran to the others. Her eyes were wide as she came running out of the tent. She ran straight for Malinter. He stood up, panicked by her reaction.

"Malinter, we need to take the tent down. Everyone has to see this," she said quickly.

Everyone grabbed the outside of the tent and pulled it away. Shala grabbed some pins and placed them on the tent sheet against the tree. Akatila took her place beside Chezuv once more, placing her hand over his forehead. The memory began to project loud and clear. Everyone stood there watching and waiting.

"Hey, Malinter, I'm going out for an errand. Watch over the camp while I am gone. I shouldn't be gone exceedingly long," Chezuv said calmly.

"Alright but be careful," Malinter replied.

Chezuv left the camp as quietly as he always had. He made his way down the path heading toward town. ShadowCry Forest was oddly quiet. He came to the fork in the path. Left was the way to town; right was to an unknown. Chezuv turned right and made his way down the path. He noticed two men were following him. Their kimonos were the same, pure black with an outline of a dark red. He continued down the path despite knowing he was being followed. He came to a little cottage that was half burnt down. He looked back behind him to notice that the two men were no longer behind him. Chezuv was no fool. He entered the abandoned cottage and glared at the person standing there. He said nothing as the other person finally turned around.

"Akatila, is that—?" Malinter growled.

"Hush and watch!" she muttered.

He nodded and looked back at the memory playing on the sheet. She quickly glanced around to see everyone completely shocked as they would have never known that this person was capable of hurting Chezuv.

"Chezuv, it's wonderful to see you again." She snickered.

"I wish I could say the same thing about you, Esmelina," he said hurtfully.

"Oh, come on, Chezuv, you still can't be cross with me? That was a long time ago. I had no choice but to leave you. I did not want you getting hurt or paying the price for something I had done," she said, looking at him.

Chezuv did not meet her gaze. She sighed and sat down at the little table in the middle of the room. He remained by the door. The two men appeared behind Esmelina. She looked at Chezuv with hurt and regret in her eyes. She sniffled as tears began to fall down her cheeks. Chezuv finally looked closer at her.

"Where is she?" Chezuv growled coldly.

"Oh darn, you finally figured out it was not your precious lover. Shucks, I thought I played her very well," Nakamyomi snickered, standing up.

Akatila growled and narrowed her eyes at the sheet. Everyone gasped but she saw Malinter looked slightly relieved that it was someone different. She figured she would ask later. She looked at Chezuv, who was still unconscious, and sighed before looking back at the memory.

Nakamyomi snapped her fingers and five guys jumped from behind

Chezuv, knocking him to the ground. They kicked and hit him until they knocked him out. They dragged him a few miles north to a small camp, where she had him tied up to a wooden post in a cell. The men continued to beat Chezuv until she entered the cell. Chezuv looked at her but could barely focus on her. His eyes were swollen and he was covered in blood. He coughed and spit up some blood as he glared at her.

"So now are you going to tell me what I want to know? Or can I just kill you?" she asked.

"Depends, what do you want to know? If it is how to find a heart and some beauty tips, I am not the guy you're looking for." He snickered before coughing again.

She backhanded him, causing him to wince again from the pain. He looked back at her and smirked before spitting some blood on her face and then chuckled weakly. She growled, wiping the blood away and nodding to the guard, who hit Chezuv so hard it dislocated his right shoulder. He finally yelled out from the pain.

"Oh, that is right, you do not know! Oh, here, let me lift your spirits some." Nakamyomi laughed.

A guard brought in another prisoner. She was covered in bruises and cut marks. Her hair was down but Chezuv knew that scent, he knew the prisoner. He whined softly as the person looked up slightly. Despite hardly being able to see, he knew it was Esmelina. He could see her beautiful blue eyes forming with tears.

"Chezuv!" she cried out, trying to get to him.

"Esmelina?" he coughed.

She struggled to get to him but the guard held her tightly. She looked at him completely beaten and destroyed. She knew he could last a long time but she could not stand to see him like this. He looked away from her as she looked at the ground. The guard took her back to her cell. Nakamyomi stood in front of Chezuv, grinning ear to ear.

"Now how about a deal?" she suggested calmly.

"What?" he winced.

"Information for the freedom of Esmelina. She's been a prisoner of mine for many years, I am sure you want her to be safe," she said, playing with his emotions.

"Despite my love for her, I will not tell you what you want to know," he grimaced.

"Chezuv, you do not know what I want yet," she said, confused.

He chuckled and then groaned from the pain. She growled, leaving him alone. He thought about how he'd been told Esmelina was dead and that he would never see her again. He knew he had to get out but he also knew he could not take her; he did not have that kind of strength. He passed out from the pain. He knew come the following day he had to break out and get back to the others. He dreamt of seeing his friends and brother again, he dreamt of having a family with the love of his life. His dream was short-lived as he woke up to cold water being thrown at him. He gasped awake and shivered from the cold. He glared at Nakamyomi. She chuckled, leaving him again.

"Okay, this is my chance," he said to himself.

He looked at his hands knowing this would hurt. He looked at the rope and began to chew through it. The water from the ropes rubbed against his hands, causing them to bleed. He knew he had to break free. After a little while of trying he finally got through and the ropes snapped. He fell to the ground. He struggled to get up. He staggered out of the cell. He saw some guards coming his way and he ducked behind a wall. When he saw it Emelina's cell, he ran to her but she was so badly hurt. He gently pushed her hair back. She flinched until she noticed who it was and she whimpered softly.

"I will come back for you," he promised.

She nodded. He kissed her lips softly. It broke his heart to have finally found her and then having to leave her behind. He was not sure if she would still be here when he came back for her, but he would not let her go again. He ducked out of the cell when he heard the guards yelling that he had escaped.

Nakamyomi came running, passing him without even knowing it. He got outside of the small camp and shifted. He began to run but he barely had any strength. He knew it would be a long way back to his camp and there would be hell to pay from his friends and family.

He ran through ShadowCry Forest staggering. He had two soldiers running after him, but someone saved him again. He saw a glimpse of white tiger. He knew who it was but he was confused about how. He kept running until he got to the camp. He shifted and could hear everyone arguing.

"Malinter! Be reasonable! You will not be able to find him tonight! Wait until the morning. We will separate into teams and find him," Ze snapped.

"I do not care if it is dark or not! I must find him! My brother has never been gone for two days!" Malinter challenged.

"Both of you stop it!" Akatila pleaded.

She turned around, hearing someone approaching them. Chezuv looked at Akatila but he knew she could not see him, only smell him. She let out a small growl. He then realized he was downwind so she could not smell him. He knew if he walked any farther without being seen they would likely attack. He stepped a bit closer until everyone turned around, staring into the darkness of the forest. Malinter narrowed his eyes.

Akatila removed her hand, ending the memory as they had caught up till they found him outside the camp. Akatila looked to Malinter, who was in shock. Akatila was exhausted and drained from using her power for so long. Shala nodded to her and then checked on Chezuv, who was beginning to respond to the herbal remedies.

"Malinter, he is finally responding. He should wake up in the morning," Shala said, relieved.

He nodded with relief as well but said nothing as he tried to process what he was just shown. He looked to Akatila, who was barely awake. She was pale in the face before he realized she had been using her power for that long with no break. He sighed, smiling gently at her.

CHAPTER ELEVEN

After the memory ended, everyone was silent and still in shock. No one could believe what they just saw. Akatila was exhausted from it. Riku picked her up and put her in his bed gently. He quietly left as she fell asleep quickly. He met the others outside. No one spoke until Malinter finally spoke up, causing everyone to jump.

"We need to go after her. We need to find her. She is one of us. I thought she was dead," Malinter said quickly.

"Malinter, we want to but we do not know if she is even still there or if she is even still alive. We do not even know where they were held. We should wait until Chezuv wakes up, he can tell us more," Sprin spoke up.

Akatila woke up. She looked around the tent to see there was no one in there but her. She snuck out of the tent and went back to Chezuv, curious about something. She began to search through his most recent memories, looking for any clue. When she saw a white tiger, she crossed her eyebrows in confusion. She did not know anyone with that animal. She pulled her hand back with confusion. She left the den bumping into Sprin. Sprin saw Akatila's facial expression and nudged Malinter. Everyone turned their attention to her yet again. She played the memory back in her head trying to figure it out. She was troubled by the white tiger, but she saw Malinter.

"Who has a white tiger?" she asked suddenly.

"Why do you ask?" Malinter said, getting defensive.

"Just answer the question!" Akatila snapped.

"Esmelina," he said softly.

Akatila went silent and walked away. Malinter tried to go after her but Chezuv began to moan a bit, so he entered the tent and sat down. Akatila returned to her tent quickly. She began to pace back and forth, thinking

92

about how to tell them what she knew. She had not the slightest idea how to explain to them that Esmelina was in fact the good person and she was just being used as a pawn to get to Chezuv, but that was not the truth. Akatila knew that Esmelina was in fact not a good person anymore and that Chezuv was in trouble.

"Okay, Akatila, how to tell them. You cannot just walk in there and tell them that she is not just a pawn and that there is someone else at hand that is trying to get back at Chezuv for something when they were younger. But then again, I cannot just tell them that there is no chance that she will stick around once we find her, if we find her," she muttered to herself.

She groaned and returned to the others to find everyone sitting outside. She was confused and rushed over to them. She did a quick head count and noticed that Shala and Malinter must be inside still.

"I need more herbs. If he is to wake up soon, he will need them," she said softly.

"I will go get them," Sprin said quickly.

"I will go too," Akatila piped in, Shala nodded and wrote down quickly what she would need and where to find them. As they walked away from the tent, Shala noticed Chezuv was twitching and she knew it would be soon.

They gathered their things and made to leave the camp but Riku stopped them.

"Be safe, you two." He smiled softly.

"We will," she replied as they left.

Chezuv began to finally wake up; however, his wounds were still in bad shape. Shala needed other herbs to be able to heal this. She knew that they would not be back in time. She had no choice but to use her powers. It was to save a family member, so she did not care about the toll it would take on her. She gently placed her hand over his leg, mending the broken bones quickly. She moved her hands over his stomach and rib cage, reconstructing his ribcage and getting rid of any internal bleeding and bruising. She felt everything mend as she continued to his arms. She knew this was one of the worst areas for him. She sighed and began to work on him.

Meanwhile, Sprin and Akatila had set out in hopes of finding the herbs that Shala needed. They knew they need to find chamomile, valerian, and ginger. They knew that some of it might be found from a local medicine man down by the river, and the rest would have to be picked up from the town market; however, they had to hurry. Chezuv could wake up at any time and be in massive pain. They knew that the man at the river may or may not be there, so they decided to head there first. They took the right at the fork in the road; however, they noticed that something was not quite right with the way they chose. Sprin looked at Akatila and shrugged. They continued down the path thinking maybe due to the fog they just did not recognize where they were.

"Um," Akatila said softly.

"Shh," Sprin said quickly.

Akatila looked around slightly confused. She knew this was the right area but maybe she was wrong. Sprin also knew that this was not the right area but he was more confused about how they could have gotten lost. They knew the way to the river and the way to town. He looked around as Akatila sat on the ground, exhausted. He walked a way for a moment, trying to see if he could find a marker or something that he would recognize. But it was hopeless.

"Are you sure this where we were supposed to be?" Akatila asked nervously.

"I thought so. Let us go back. Maybe we turned the wrong way. Who knows with this fog coming in," Sprin said calmly.

She nodded and they turned around to head back from where they came, but they were lost and they both knew it. Sprin tried to listen for anyone approaching but he could not hear a single noise. He quickly grabbed Akatila's arm and pulled her to his side. He knew there was something out there and he knew what they were after.

"Sprin, I am scared," she whimpered.

"Shh, it will be okay, I promise," he said softly.

They heard a twig break and jumped, looking behind them. The fog was getting worse but they still did not know which way to go. Now they could hear footsteps, which made Akatila nervous. She thought it could be Yukia and Miko or even Master Goenjo. She could feel her heart racing.

They tried to continue to walk away from the footsteps but they only followed Sprin and Akatila. She stopped beside Sprin. She felt the air get cold and the fog was thick. She could only think of her nightmare, as did Sprin. He placed a hand on her arm gently. She stood closely to him in fear of what could be approaching them. She could hear footsteps and she began to get nervous. It was only her and Sprin, no one else. She growled and shifted, as did Sprin, once they realized it was a scent they did not know. She growled softly. Akatila then yelped as she felt someone bite into her leg. They ran off with her.

She felt her body hitting the ground as she tried to break free. Sprin hit them from the side, forcing them to let go of her. She whimpered as she lay there. Sprin came over nudging her gently and stood protectively over her. His panther was much bigger than her small-framed fox. He knew he could protect her or die trying. He could not see where they were attacking from or how many. He heard footsteps from behind him, but when he turned to swing, he was met by deep blue eyes. He knew it was Chezuv. He then saw a snowy owl overhead and knew it was Shala. He yowled to get her attention. She flew down, shifting as she touched the ground. She hurried to Akatila's leg. She nodded to Chezuv, who was still in his animal form along with Sprin.

"Akatila this is going to burn badly," she whispered.

She nodded to Shala. She was too afraid to shift into her normal self-due to the extent of her injuries. She whimpered as Shala poured hot herbs over her leg. She flinched but tried to remain calm. She heard other footsteps approaching quickly and she whined to Sprin, who turned and jumped over them, covering them, ready to defend them. He relaxed, seeing a caracal appear. An Indian leopard and a Eurasian lynx stepped out of the fog. He knew it was Harnuq, Riku, and Angelia. He heard the screech of a hawk and knew it was Anoquv as well. He returned to Chezuv.

Everyone shifted to normal, including Akatila. Chezuv and Sprin covered one side while Harnuq and Riku covered the other. Angelia knelt beside her sister, worried. Anoquv remained in his animal form as he tried to keep an eye out.

"Who did this?" Shala finally asked.

"I am not sure, Shala, we never saw them. We smelled them and could hear them. I do not know how many there even were," she said, gritting her teeth from the pain.

"One minute she was beside me, the next she was being dragged," Sprin said cautiously.

"So did they knew who you were?" she asked.

"No, not that I know of," she winced.

Anoquv got an idea, he flew down and shifted into his human form. He began to maneuver his hands in a circle and the fog cleared. He continued gathering all the fog and sending it above the tree line. However, even with the fog gone no one could see anything. Sprin stepped up next and used his hands to project small balls of fire to the sides of them, creating a path. This time Chezuv saw someone and his heart shattered. He saw the outline of a familiar figure but this person remained in the shadows. He growled. He charged at the shadow and was able to grab them; however, Akatila could still smell her attacker nearby and Chezuv was about four miles away from her.

Anoquv suddenly got a look on his face of excitement and pure confusion. He ran off, following Chezuv. Sprin was right behind him, leaving only Riku to guard Shala, Akatila, and Angelia. Riku huffed and looked down at Akatila, who looked worried still. He bent down and kissed the top of her head gently, reassuring her that everything would be okay.

Anoquv and Sprin had caught up to Chezuv, who was standing in a small clearing. In the middle of the clearing was a young woman with long hair, big blue eyes. Anoquv knew who it was immediately.

"Hello, Chezuv," she said sweetly.

Chezuv sat there silently. He looked at her with confusion and hurt; she would not meet his gaze. He whimpered and finally she looked up at him.

"Why, Esmelina? Why would you do this to me?" he asked, hurt.

"Chezuv, I never wanted to. She told me if I did not act like a captive, she would kill you. I was just trying to protect you as I always have," she cried out.

Tears ran down her face. She knew he would never forgive her, but she also knew he knew she was telling the truth. Since he can read minds, there was no point in lying to him about it. He stood there watching her cry. His heart broke but he turned to the others and his gaze went dark and emotionless again. They grabbed onto her gently and began making their way back to camp. Raynier ran out of his tent seeing them entering camp. Seto and Greto ran to Akatila. Riku and Angelia were holding Akatila up as she was still very weak. Anoquv and Malinter had a hold of Esmelina, while everyone else sat beside the campfire.

"Get her out of here," Chezuv said softly.

"Chezuv, please," she whimpered as Malinter took her to a different tent.

There was a moment of silence in the camp as everyone stood there still shocked about what they had just heard and seen. Malinter returned and looked at Chezuv carefully. Akatila was the only one brave enough to approach Chezuv. She did so cautiously. She gently placed her hand on his arm. He snapped his head up. He stared at her. His eyes were red and puffy. Tears silently fell down his cheeks while he did not make any sound. She hugged him gently. He buried his face into her shoulder and silently cried. His heart felt like it was going to explode all over again. He'd sworn that he would not feel this again but he did.

Akatila gently ran her hand over his head and hair trying to calm him down. Malinter stood beside her with his hand gently on his brother's back. Ze and Shala were the next to approach him, one on each side of Chezuv, gently hugging him. Seto, Anoquv, and Greto were the next to follow suit, all three gently placing a hand on him to let him know they were there for him. Angelia, Riku, Raynier, Harnuq, and Sprin shook off the shock and approached the group, gently hugging the others. Chezuv felt safe and able to break. He sobbed softly. Akatila knew for that moment this was the closest everyone had been in the last few months. She was relieved but also upset that this had to happen to bring them closer as a family.

"Chezuv, maybe you should get some rest. Tomorrow we are supposed to look for our new home, remember?" Akatila whispered.

"You are right, we should all turn in," he said softly.

Everyone watched Malinter take Chezuv back to the tent before they returned to their own tents. Akatila was worried about Chezuv and about Esmelina. She did not know what would happen to her. She closed her eyes and finally drifted to sleep.

She woke up the next morning to Chezuv yelling and hearing Malinter yelling back. She rushed out to see everyone standing between them.

"What is going on?" she declared.

"Chezuv wants to let her go! I say keep her here so we can keep an eye on her," Malinter growled.

"I say let her go! If she wants to be here then she will stay. If not, let her go. She has already been a captive for one person, I will not have her go through that again!" Chezuv snapped back.

Akatila rolled her eyes and went to see Esmelina. She looked exhausted and worn down. Akatila gently placed a bowl of fresh water down for her. She looked up at Akatila, confused by the bowl. She closed her eyes and looked away. Akatila knew what she was feeling, so she sat down. She ignored the yelling coming from the courtyard.

"I used to be a captive for Master Goenjo," Akatila said softly as Esmelina looked up in surprise.

"I know what it feels like to be tortured. I know how it feels to want to cry so hard and scream so loud but you know that no one will hear you or help you. I get that it hurts. I understand how many times you have wanted the pain to end no matter the cost. And I also know it was not you who attacked me," she finished.

"How do you know such things?" Esmelina asked, her voice cracking softly.

"Your scent, it does not match the one that attacked me a few nights ago. You were not the person who bit me. I am still not sure who did." she replied calmly.

Little did Akatila know, Ze was standing outside of the tent listening. Once he heard that Esmelina was not the attacker, he knew Malinter would back off. He quickly made his way back to the group. He noticed that Malinter and Chezuv were still fighting and it was only getting worse. He quickly darted between them, causing them both to stop yelling and look at him with confusion.

"Both of you listen! Esmelina is not the person who attacked Akatila. I just overheard her talking and Akatila told Esmelina she knew she had not done the attacking, she was the savior. We messed up." Ze scowled.

Akatila came out with Esmelina, who was all cleaned up. She stood in front of Chezuv and looked at him. Her eyes were gentle and full of love for him, as his eyes softened, looking down at her. He sighed and looked away knowing she would leave and he would lose her again. He felt his heart breaking again. She gently placed a hand on his cheek and pulled his face back to her, making him look at her. She smiled gently at him as no words were spoken. She hugged him tightly. He allow the hug and secretly enjoyed it and kissed the top of her head gently.

"I know you hate me but I would never attack Akatila. I also have been told that you need a new home. There is a town that has welcomed me down at the edge of the forest. It is not too far from here. I am sure they will welcome you as well," she said softly.

"Chezuv, I know what village she is talking about. We used to go there when we were younger. The town is small but it is super cute, and most people do not even know that it is there. We might be able to have a normal life in that village. Please, can we at least check it out?" Angelia asked.

"Very well. We will go there now. As for you, you may come with us or leave. Whichever you chose," Chezuv said softly to Esmelina.

Everyone grabbed their things from their tents and made their way to the village at the end of the forest. Everyone began to talk about the things that they could do with a normal life—have a family, get married, find love. Anoquv was eager to find a girlfriend, as was Seto, who had finally come around to the idea of feelings. Akatila knew that Shala and Ze would have kids someday, so why not in a village that is peaceful and safe. She giggled at the thought of kids. She glanced over to Raynier as he looked back at her with a soft smile. He walked over to Anoquv and Seto and began talking about girlfriends.

"And what is so funny, sweets?" Riku asked, coming from behind her.

"Nothing," she replied innocently.

"Nothing's nothing," he replied, smirking.

"Ever thought of having kids one day, Riku? You know, having little ones running around a house filled with laughter and love?" she asked.

"Of course, I have, only with you though," he replied, kissing her softly.

They finally got to the edge of the forest and noticed the small village. Akatila and Angelia were both excited to be back in a place they used to know. It was exciting for everyone.

As they went down the hill, Esmelina pulled Chezuv to the side. There was worry in her eyes.

"Esmelina, is everything okay?" Chezuv questioned.

"No, not really. You must know that there is another person involved in this, Chezuv. It is just not Master Goenjo and the king, there is a third person. I am not sure who but it is whoever took us away all those years ago. This person, Chezuv, they are planning something big. Please, please be careful," she begged.

"I will try my best to be careful," he said softly.

He gently brushed her hair out of her eyes. He smiled, looking into them, as he kissed her lips softly. She smiled within the kiss knowing he would be okay if she was not around. Wherever she went, people she loved always got hurt. He knew that and he nodded to her.

"I will be back one day," she whispered as she ran into the shadows.

When he turned around everyone was making their way into the town already. He glanced back and Esmelina was nowhere to be found. He sighed but he joined the others. Akatila was already speaking with the towns elders about perhaps finding a home. He knew that she would be able to make it work, everyone loved her. Chezuv decided to walk around the town, his mind was on Esmelina. He wished she had stayed, but he knew why she had left again. Malinter went and found Chezuv and sighed. He placed a hand on his brother's shoulder.

"You might want to come see this." Malinter said softly.

He nodded and followed his brother. Chezuv gasped softly as he noticed that the townsfolk had already set them up with little houses of their own and were showing the others to them. He knew this was Akatila's doing and he smiled. He walked over and noticed Akatila was nowhere to be found. Riku smirked and pointed to a small field and he could hear her giggling with some children.

CHAPTER TWELVE

She gave out a small giggle as she lay down with some of the children from the town. They lay in the field of daisies. One of the little girls pounced on Akatila, making her squeak. The little girl just giggled, cuddling against her. The other kids curled up beside Akatila. She smiled looking at them. She knew that they were so pure, they had no idea what was going on the outside world. She sighed as she played with the little girl's hair softly.

"Can you sing for us?" the little girl asked as she fell asleep.

"Of course," she smiled.

It had been so long since she had sung for anyone, she had to think of what to sing. She then had a memory flash in her head of a song her mother used to sing to her. She began to hum as the kids got even closer to her. She had the little girl falling asleep on her lap, while two fell asleep at her feet, one on each of her side, and then another one passed out across her legs.

"As the sun rises, know I am here, my little one. As the sun sets, never fear for I am here. Sounds of the day fade away, the stars come out to play. Reach for them, my little one, for they are bright. Know that you are safe right here in my arms, and it will always feel right," she sang softly.

Little did she know that her sister and everyone else were behind her, listening. Angelia smiled as it had been a lifetime since her sister sang. She swayed with the tunes her sister sang and she knew it was her mother's song Akatila was singing. But how did they know that? It just felt right. She leaned against Harnuq as Seto approached slowly. He did not want to wake any of the kids or disturb Akatila.

"My love is always with you near or far. Here in arms you can dream and shine brighter than the stars. How sweet to hold you, how gentle and fragile your love is. As the sun rises, know I am here, my little one. As the sun sets, never fear for I am here. Sounds of the waves crash, the wind plays in the trees. Remember, my little one, the best things come in threes," Akatila continued the song.

She realized all the children were asleep and she let out a small little giggle before hearing everyone yawning from behind her. She looked over her shoulder to see everyone and she just blushed. She had never sung for them before, neither did she know that they were there. She gently moved each little one before getting up and going to them. Angelia looked at her sister and hugged her gently. Seto just smiled at his sisters before looking to Riku.

"I did not know you could sing, Akatila. You should do it more often," Riku said shyly.

"I do not even know where that came from, it just felt right." She shrugged.

"It was a song your mother used to sing to you three every night, especially if there was thunder and lightning," Greto said, walking to them with tears in his eyes. "You sang it just as beautifully as she used to," Greto whispered.

Akatila looked back at the sleeping children. She knew what each of those kids was going through without a parent in their life. She knew even if it were just a lullaby at least it gave them a sense of what life should be like. She looked away and looked back at Greto. She opened her mouth but the question would not come out. Angelia knew that her sister was very curious about their mother. She decided to ask for her sister.

"Hey, Dad? What was our mother like?" Angelia asked softly.

Greto for a moment was stunned, he was still not used to hearing the word dad come from his daughter. He shook his head shaking it off.

"You're mom?" He sighed softly, sitting down.

Everyone sat down as they were all curious to know what Akatila's mom was like. Angelia lay against Harnuq. Anoquv, Sprin, Malinter, and Chezuv sat on tree stumps, while Shala curled up against Ze. The rare occasion that Ze would smile is when Shala is around and beside him. Akatila giggled until she felt arms around her. She looked back and saw Riku, and she snuggled up against him. Raynier watched the children to make sure they were still safe. Greto looked at everyone and gave a small smile, seeing for once there was no fighting, there were no battles. For once it seemed peaceful.

"Their mom, oh boy, she was such a handful when we were kids. She always used to get into trouble. I always had to get her out of it. I remember this one time, we were playing in the town square and she got caught by the shopkeeper. The shopkeeper made her clean the shop every day for a week because she had broken a fragile piece of pottery. Little did the shopkeeper know she never did it. I went every day and did it for her. I did not want her to be a slave to someone who was such a jerk." He chuckled.

"So you were Mom's best friend?" Seto chimed in.

"We were best friends since birth. Our moms were best friends. Me and their mother grew up together, same little town, same school, same friends. We were inseparable. That is, until I got older. I got drafted into the first battle of this war. Your mother was so worried I would not come back. I remember seeing her the first day I came back home. She was still as beautiful as the first day I realized I loved her. She ran to me just crying, excited to see I was okay." He sighed, closing his eyes for a moment.

"What was her name? You know, Mom's name?" Akatila whispered.

"Your mother's name? Nevaeh, it's *heaven* spelled backward." He smiled saying it.

Akatila smiled knowing her mother's name as she thought about what her mother looked like. Her father says she looks just like her mother, so she wondered if maybe they could be twins by how close they looked alike. She wondered if her mother was proud of her. She missed her mom so much but tried not to show it. She snapped out of her thoughts when she heard her name mentioned and she wondered why,

"When Akatila was extraordinarily little she was determined to walk. There was a point where Seto was so protective over her that he refused to let her walk. Once Angelia was born, he became so protective over the two that I could not have been prouder. Until one day . . ." He paused.

"Until what day?" Harnuq shouted.

"We were all in the town market. Angelia was still a baby, Seto was about six years old and Akatila was about four. There was a girl that was crushing on Seto badly. She would follow him everywhere he went. Well, one day Akatila I guess had had enough and walked over to Seto and asked for help. When he helped her it made the other girl mad. Akatila stuck her tongue out at her and snickered. The girl got mad and pushed Seto by accident. Akatila walked up to the girl and punched her right in the nose, walked to Seto, helped him up, and gave him her candy that I had bought her. It was so funny. I was laughing so hard. Neveah, however, was not impressed. She was mad that Akatila had hit her for no reason," Greto said, laughing.

Both Seto and Akatila were so red from embarrassment. She shrank into Riku, who was also laughing. Seto dove behind the tree trunk. Angelia just laughed and laughed, as everyone did, it was one of the few times they could just laugh and not worry.

"Hey, Akatila is still that way! She punched a guy a long time ago for flirting with Angelia!" Ze called out.

"Hey! Do not be throwing me in the mix! Angelia loves Harnuq, no other guys need her. And really? Coming from you? Mr. Don't Even Look at Shala!" she teased.

Ze went silent as he nodded, knowing that it was a true statement. Shala giggled at him and kissed him softly before looking back to Angelia, who was laughing. Akatila ran at Angelia and jumped on her. Angelia squeaked from under her as Akatila began to tickle her sister. Seto jumped from behind the tree trunk to recuse Angelia. As he batted Akatila away, Riku jumped to her defense and started batting back at Seto. Chezuv and Malinter were laughing watching the two smack each other's hands like schoolgirls would in a fight. Greto smiled as he stopped talking about their mother; he just seemed to be lost in thought. Angelia gave Harnuq a soft kiss on his cheek and smiled up at him before she cuddled back into him. Akatila giggled at her sister, making Seto throw a blanket at Akatila.

"No picking on Angelia!" he chuckled.

"So much for no favorites, huh?" she scoffed, smiling.

Seto smiled over to Angelia. Everyone knew Angelia was Seto's favorite. Meanwhile, Greto snuck over to Akatila and grabbed the blanket. He waited until Seto was no longer paying attention, which did not take long as he thought he was untouchable. Greto tossed the same blanket back at Seto, catching him off guard, making him fall off the tree stump, landing on the ground. He shook his head as he shot a playful glare at Akatila and stuck his tongue out at her pouting. Angelia was laughing so hard she was crying.

"No picking on your sister!" Greto chuckled.

Akatila laughed knowing who the favorite daughter and sibling was now. Riku ran his fingers through her hair, making her relax again as Chezuv brought everyone a small cup of herbal tea. The wind began to pick up, making it seem colder than it was. She sipped on the tea and it warmed her up again. She gave another giggle as she became lost in thought.

"Now I know why you think I am a lot like Mom." Akatila gave a little giggle.

"You are a lot like your mom in more ways than one," he said softly.

She looked at her father in confusion as he got up and walked away. She tapped Riku and he let go of her. She chased after him as everyone sat there in confusion. Angelia looked around at everyone and could see that no one knew what her father meant. She looked at her brother and she knew he knew what Greto meant. She got up from Harnuq and walked over to Seto, who was staring at the ground. She nudged him, making him look up at her.

"You know what Dad meant by that?" she asked.

"He almost lost Mom to someone else a long time ago. I do not know who but she chose Dad over the other guy. He sees Mom in Akatila because of Riku and Raynier," he replied softly so no one else heard.

Meanwhile, Akatila chased after her dad. She found him down by the stream. She sighed with relief as she approached him. She sat next to him as he stared into the water. She gave him a nudge gently. He smiled at her before finally speaking.

"I loved your mother very much and I miss her every day," he said softly.

"I wish I knew her. I know I miss her," she replied.

"I stole your mother," he muttered.

"I am sorry, what?" She shook her head.

"Not like that. Your mother was engaged to another man. But we grew up together, we were in love. Her father did not approve of me, arranged for her to be married to someone else. She hated the other man. I never met him, and she never told me who it was. She met me by the river on the outside of town one night. We ran. We ran and never looked back. We built a great home, had three amazing kids. The day I lost you kids I felt my heart break. When I realized your mother was taken as well, I felt like I had died. I do not want you to be in the same place, Akatila. I know that Riku and Raynier both love you, please do not lead them on. Please choose and figure it out. I don't want to lose you also," Greto said softly.

Greto returned to everyone, leaving Akatila there. Riku came out from the shadows and sat down beside her. He nudged her gently. She glanced beside her and smiled softly as she was still lost in thought. She knew they both liked her, but she also knew who she loved. But how could she say it?

She leaned against Riku as she continued to think. He gently held her as he rubbed her back to keep her calm. He kissed the top of her head gently.

Something ran past them, making them both jump their feet. Riku pushed Akatila behind him gently but kept a hand gently on her shirt.

"Miss me?" a voice spoke from the shadows.

Akatila began to tremble as she knew that voice but she knew she had to put on a front that he did not bother her. It killed her to know that someone she loved so much was betraying her like this, had hurt her so much physically and mentally. She refused to look at him.

Riku growled in warning as Yukia got closer. Yukia smirked, seeing Akatila's reaction.

"Aw what's wrong, sweets? Cannot face me? Love me too much?" he snickered.

"*Loved*, you are right. I used to love you when we were kids. I still do not understand why you are doing this," she whispered.

"You loved him?" Riku said, shocked.

Riku backed up from Akatila, his eyes were wide with shock. She didn't move as hatred filled her. She could feel her heart breaking knowing he now hated her.

"A long time ago when we were kids, yes. He was my best friend. He was my everything," she replied, heartbroken.

"Ah yes, young love. Such a waste," Yukia replied, sneering.

"We end this now, Yukia!" Riku growled, shifting, and charging at him.

Yukia smirked, shifting, and running off. He knew that if he killed Riku, Akatila would be weak enough for him to kill as well. He knew he had to lead Riku to the cliffs but he would have a little fun first. Yukia dipped and ducked under the large tree trunks that stuck out of the ground. He leaped over branches knowing that Riku would have a hard time keeping up since a leopard is not as small as a fox is.

Yukia finally got Riku to trip up and hit the ground. He sat on the edge of a tree trunk. He snickered, letting out a cackle to taunt him. Riku got to his paws again and chased after him. He led Riku to the cliffs finally, except he thought he could sneak around him. When he realized he was trapped; it was too late. He shifted back to himself, as did Riku, who was furious, his warm gaze was cold. Yukia knew he did not stand a chance in human form against Riku.

"Just give up, Yukia! You have nowhere to run this time. It is just you and I," Riku said coldly.

Yukia looked around for a way out of this. He soon realized there was no way out unless he jumped into the ocean below. He glanced over the edge and then looked back at Riku and smirked. He jumped over the edge into the water. Riku ran to the edge but never saw Yukia emerge. He closed his eyes as he felt a small part of him that was upset for losing someone he used to consider a friend. He turned away, leaving the cliff and Yukia behind.

CHAPTER THIRTEEN

Yukia emerged from the water coughing and gasping. He looked up from where he fell and sighed with relief that he was alive. He knew he had to get back to the camp and tell Miko what was going on and where they could be found. He staggered a bit as his body still stung from the water. He continued to walk until he got somewhere familiar and shifted and ran back to the camp.

He finally arrived, seeing two soldiers guarding the camp. They drew their katanas in wait.

"Easy, it is me," Yukia said, shifting to himself.

"Where have you been?" Miko exclaimed at seeing the young man.

"I know where they are hiding Akatila. I saw and spoke with her," Yukia said coldly.

Miko nodded as he listened to Yukia's story on how things went between him, Akatila, and Riku. He grinned to know that Yukia had maybe put doubt in Riku's mind. Yukia sat beside the fire trying to warm up and dry off. Miko dropped some fresh clothes beside him before returning to his tent. Yukia raised an eyebrow in confusion but changed into some dry clothes and returned to his tent as well.

"I cannot believe you loved him at some point! Do you still do?" Riku said, hurt.

"I loved him a long time ago when we were kids growing up. After he left me on the battlefield, I knew he was no longer my friend," she said, tears filling her eyes.

They entered the part of town where they lived still yelling at each other, drawing everyone out from their homes, including Angelia and

Raynier. Angelia and Seto ran to their sister, worried about why she was crying and why Riku was so furious at her. Akatila saw her sister and ran to her, burying her face into her sister's chest, sobbing. Seto glared at Riku but he saw the hurt in his eyes.

"Sweets, what is wrong? What happened?" Raynier asked, approaching slowly.

"Yukia happened!" she exclaimed.

"Sweets, talk to us. What happened with Yukia?" Raynier asked, kneeling beside Angelia and Akatila.

"He came back. He tried to get in my head, but when I would not fall for his tricks, he got inside Riku's head! And now Riku thinks I am still in love with Yukia! And he hates me!" she said, gasping for air in between her sobs.

The group went silent as Riku returned to his home heartbroken. Chezuv glared as he knew who was really behind this. He nudged Malinter as they turned to the shadows. Greto was right with them as was Ze. They stood around a small tree stump that was barely poking out of the ground. In front of them was a small bed of daisies and roses at the bottom of the stump.

"What do we do? What did Riku do to Yukia?" Ze asked first.

"I am not sure. However, I do know that Yukia is alive, Miko is behind this, and there is something bigger planned. There is no way that Miko would send Yukia to Akatila just to get inside her head. He wanted her weakened, but for what?" Chezuv replied.

"Chezuv, what if this has to do with the king? Do we just forget that Miko is just his puppet and so is Master Goenjo? Do we forget about Master Goenjo as well and just focus on these two?" Malinter questioned.

All four of them went silent as they tried to think of what the plan could be for doing this. They tried to think of what the purpose was for sending him, but none of them could come to a reason. Malinter shook his head but took a stance at hearing someone approach. Ze backed up into the shadows until he recognized the scent. It was Shala. She stepped out from the shadows with a small grin on her face as she looked at them all before bowing slowly. Ze stepped up beside her and kissed her head gently.

"Chezuv, I wish to go into town and get a few things. Maybe a small party tonight might help brighten the day . . . well, the night technically." She giggled.

"Very well, I think that will be a great idea. With everything that has happened in the last few months, a night of good times and laughter will be great for everyone. Take some others with you just in case," Chezuv said, smiling.

She nodded as she returned to the others and saw Anoquv, Raynier, and Angelia. She approached the three as they were talking about Akatila and Riku. She stood a bit back so she could listen to them without being spotted.

"Listen, I know you all know that I love Akatila. However, I do understand that her heart belongs to Riku. How could he just hurt her like that? And believing Yukia of all people!" Raynier said coldly.

"I am not sure why he would believe him. Her feelings for him are beyond noticeable. Or at least for us it is truly clear. Perhaps he just needs to be reminded of that?" Angelia said, questioning.

"Perhaps, but how?" Anoquv asked her.

Shala stepped forward, giggling softly, making all three of them jump. They relaxed seeing it was only Shala and not Akatila. Shala stood beside Angelia before looking to Raynier. Hurt covered his eyes but there was a glimmer of happiness as well. She sighed before speaking.

"Tonight, Chezuv wants to have somewhat of a party-type thing, food, dancing. Maybe before that it would be a great idea to get the two in the same tent and let them talk," Shala suggested.

They all nodded and were curious about what Shala had up her sleeve. She laughed at them and walked away. Soon they realized she was going into town and chased after her. They made their way into the town square. Shala grabbed what she needed, as did the others.

Meanwhile, Akatila came out of her house to see Riku coming out of his. She whimpered as she wiped the tears from her cheek. He looked over at her and sighed, approaching her.

"Akatila," he said softly.

"How could you believe him? How could you think that I loved him when it is clear who I love? Do I not make it clear enough?" she asked quickly.

He groaned as he knew she was getting upset all over again. He did what he knew to do when she was like this. He stepped forward, sliding his hand around the back of her neck gently, and pulled her to him, kissing her gently. She relaxed and deepened the kiss before hugging him.

Shala and the others had returned with some food and decorations. She began setting the food up while Angelia hung some lights around the outside of the houses. Harnuq and Anoquv set the wood into the fire pit and lit it. Chezuv and Malinter both chuckled seeing Ze and Shala dancing together.

Everyone sat around the fire as the sun finally set.

"Are we okay?" Riku asked her nervously.

"We are perfect. Now let's go have some fun." She smiled.

Everyone laughed and danced as the fire flickered. Akatila and Riku had made up and were dancing together as Raynier watched on. He could only chuckle and smile as he watched her. Harnuq and Angelia remained sitting beside the tree, watching everyone. Angelia began to finally eat some of the meat that was on her plate, which she had been avoiding. She felt her stomach turn but ignored it. She laughed as Akatila approached her, putting her hand out, bowing.

"Kind lady, may I have this dance?" Akatila giggled.

"Why of course!" Angelia said sarcastically.

Akatila smirked and grabbed her sister's hand anyway and dragged her out by the fire and forced her to dance. Angelia laughed as she and Akatila tried to dance but neither of them could keep rhythm long enough. Harnuq and Riku both were laughing so hard they never noticed that Chezuv and Malinter were sneaking up behind them. Harnuq and Riku both screamed as Chezuv and Malinter jumped out from the shadows, scaring them. Chezuv nudged Harnuq as Angelia was coming back toward them just giggling. She fell into Harnuq's arms exhausted from dancing. He looked at her nervously.

"Angel, can we talk?" he whispered.

"Of course, are you okay?" she said quickly.

"Yes, I am fine, but I have something I need to ask you," he said, leading her away from the others.

"Harnuq, what is going on?" she asked, confused.

"There really is no right time to say this or to ask this. However, with everything we have gone through these last few months, between Akatila taking your place, your father and brother being alive, the constant fighting and battles everywhere we go, I am worried I might lose you. And because I am worried, I have also learned that life is too short, especially for us. So I'm asking you now," he stammered.

He got down on one knee in front of her nervously. His eyes glistened with love and worry. He knew he was sweating and shaking as he pulled a small ring out of his pocket. The ring was nothing fancy, just some wood twisted into a circle. But within the wood there were pieces of rose petals and lilies. Angelia felt her eyes water as she was becoming more and more excited about what he had to ask, but she knew what the question was at this point.

"Angelia Ray, will you be my wife?" he said shyly.

"YES!" she exclaimed.

She smiled as she hugged him. He gently picked her up and spun her around excitedly. He kissed her softly before putting her back down. When he looked at her, she was still smiling but there was something in her eyes that was worrying him. He gently placed his hand under her chin and lifted her head so he would meet her gaze. He knew suddenly what was wrong. He let out a soft sigh before smiling at her. She looked at him and smiled.

"We will tell her together. For now, let us go celebrate!" He smiled.

They walked back to the fire and to everyone. Akatila was missing, so Angelia sighed softly with relief. She sat beside Shala with a huge grin on her face. Shala only gave a little giggle before looking to Harnuq, who was glowing as well. Shala had her suspicions but she dared not ask.

Everyone began to head to their tents as it was getting late. Angelia followed Harnuq into their den. Akatila finally showed up in time to say goodnight. Angelia and Harnuq sat down on the bed and began to think about how they wanted to do this celebration and where it should happen. Angelia let out a yawn before lying against Harnuq.

"Get some sleep, my love. You are going to need it," he said softly as he laid her down gently.

"Tomorrow is going to be a great day. I hope everything goes well," she whispered, half asleep.

Angelia woke up the next morning and felt sick. She figured it was some of the food they had the night before, so she went to find Shala in hopes of getting medicine for it. She left the tent quietly as everyone was still asleep. The sun had not yet risen. She tripped over a branch outside of Shala's den, alerting her.

"Angelia is everything okay?" she asked softly.

"Not really, I woke up feeling sick," Angelia replied.

Shala looked at her and nodded before entering the tent. She began to make an herbal tea to help settle her stomach but Angelia ran back out. She got outside and began to throw up. Angelia took a deep breath and shook her head. She placed her right hand on her head and her left hand on her stomach. When she turned around, Shala was standing there with a large grin on her face. Shala let out a small giggle and returned to the tent.

"Shala, what is it?" Angelia asked, concerned.

"Something wonderful and also something scary," She replied gently.

From all the noise, Harnuq entered the tent to find Angelia there. He looked at her concerned as Shala just continued to smile. Ze had also entered the tent to check on Shala. He looked at Angelia, whose face was very pale. He glanced at Shala and nodded. Ze cracked a small smile before leaving to find Chezuv. Shala turned back to face Angelia, who now looked very worried. Her face had gone pale from not feeling well. She helped Angelia sit back down on the bed and handed her a cup of water.

"Harnuq, please wait outside," she asked him.

He nodded and left.

"Angelia, do you know why you are feeling sick?" Shala asked gently.

"No, I figured it was from the food. I am wrong, aren't I?" Angelia replied slowly.

"You are very wrong, my dear, you are with child," Shala said, thrilled.

Angelia felt her heart race. She was unsure whether to be excited or scared. She did not know how Harnuq would react either or the camp or Akatila. She gulped and shrank back as she heard footsteps approaching the tent. She knew it was Ze with Chezuv. Harnuq was still sitting outside. Shala gently placed a hand on her shoulder and smiled. Angelia sighed, knowing everything would be okay. She just had to tell everyone and then go from there.

"Shala, what if Akatila hates the baby? What if Harnuq does not want the baby?" Angelia said softly as tears filled her eyes.

"Everything will be okay. We are all here for you. And as for Harnuq, I am sure he will be thrilled. Akatila, well, I am not sure about her. But you are sisters, I am sure she will be happy for you," Shala said hesitantly.

"Shala, you sent for me?" Chezuv said before entering the tent.

"You may come in, Chezuv." She giggled.

Chezuv entered the tent quietly, confusion covered his eyes as he was unsure as to why he was needed so early in the morning but he knew it had to be important. Shala gave him some tea to help him wake up just as she had given Ze and Harnuq but not Angelia. He looked at Angelia, who was still very pale in the face with concern. He looked at Shala, who stood there with a smile on her face.

"Anyone know where Akatila is this morning?" Shala asked randomly.

"She is out hunting, why?" Chezuv replied.

"Perhaps you should do a quick meeting before she gets back. Everyone should know, but Akatila should find out from Angelia," she stated.

"Find out what?" Harnuq spoke up, confused.

"I am with child," Angelia said excitedly.

"Are you really?" Harnuq asked.

"Yes, she is." Shala called out.

He picked Angelia up and spun her around in excitement. He was thrilled to hear this news. Chezuv shook his hand before calling everyone to meeting by the fire pit.

Chezuv called a quick meeting with the rest of the group and let them know what was going on. However, no one could tell Akatila until Angelia had the chance to speak with her. Everyone became excited at the thought of a new addition to the group; they were thrilled to be looking forward to something so wonderful and such a blessing. Akatila returned from hunting with a few rabbits, a squirrel, and a pigeon. She looked at everyone, confused about why they were staring at her. She put the animals down carefully before going over to everyone.

"Okay, what is going on? You guys are starting to make me worry. What happened while I was gone?" Akatila asked concerned.

No one answered her, only stared at her. She then noticed that Angelia was not to be found and her heart began to race a mile a minute as thoughts flooded her head if maybe Angelia had gotten hurt at some point, or worse, she had been kidnapped. Angelia stepped out from around everyone with Harnuq, Akatila sighed with relief but confusion still consumed her as to what was going on.

"Sis, please sit down," Angelia asked softly.

"No, I think I am okay. What is going on?" Akatila asked.

Everyone was still very silent. Akatila began to wonder if it was about a mission or if something had happened while she was gone. Maybe they had learned the whereabouts of Miko. She became excited, which gave Angelia high hopes that when she finally said it Akatila would remain happy. But somehow Angelia knew that would not be the case.

"Akatila, we have something to tell you," Angelia said nervously.

Akatila turned to look at her sister, who was standing beside Harnuq. She looked at them confused but nodded to them. She turned completely around, turning her back to the fire. The entire group went silent, which made Akatila even more nervous.

"Angelia are you okay?" she quickly asked.

"Yes, I am fine. It is nothing bad. I just do not know how you will react when I tell you," Angelia stammered. "Akatila, we have big news," she said, now with a smile. "We are getting married," Angelia said excitedly.

Akatila's jaw dropped and anger arose in her. She stood up and turned her back to her sister. Angelia shrank back as Seto had had enough of this already. He growled, approaching Akatila, and nudged her, trying to keep his cool. She glared at Seto and Greto, who had appeared beside Angelia and Harnuq. The entire group was staring at her, waiting for her to say something.

"Wait, are you serious?" Akatila asked.

"Yes. Harnuq asked me to marry him last night. Seto and Greto are happy for us. Are you?" she asked nervously.

Akatila glared coldly at her sister and Harnuq before turning her back again and attempting to leave but decided to speak her mind. She turned around and looked at her sister. Angelia met Akatila's cold gaze with only sympathy in her eyes. Harnuq growled, warning Akatila not to start something. Everyone also knew that Angelia was with child except Akatila.

"Is there anything else?" Akatila snapped.

"I am with child," Angelia replied softly.

CHAPTER FOURTEEN

"I cannot believe you! How could do something like this?" Akatila screeched at her sister.

"I am sorry that I am in love and you cannot decide who you want! That is your problem! How is Harnuq and I getting married next spring such a bad thing? Would it not be a better time? Would it not be a time to celebrate? Why can't you just be happy for me?" Angelia spat.

Akatila looked taken back by her sister's words. She glared at her sister and turned her back to her. Angelia stood there, her eyes wide. She could not believe Akatila was being like this. Harnuq placed his hand gently on Angelia's shoulder before they both turned away from her and walked away. Akatila cried silently. She knew what was going to happen and there was nothing she could do to stop it. Riku appeared in front of her and smiled at her gently. He softly wiped the tears from falling down her cheek. She hugged him and cried into his shoulder. He wrapped his arms around her, helping her calm down.

Raynier watched from a distance knowing he stood no chance against Riku. He felt his heart break not only for him but also for Angelia.

She finally pulled back from the hug and looked up at him before giving a soft smile. He kissed her forehead and walked away.

"What was that?" Seto growled, appearing from the shadows.

"What was what?" Akatila asked, confused.

"Seriously! Why must you always be such a jerk to her?" Seto defended Angelia.

Akatila looked down and turned her back to her brother and walked away to clear her head. She was the only one who knew the truth. She knew that if her sister married Harnuq all hell would break lose at that gathering. She remembered her dream about Sprin getting hurt and how that turned out. She could not guarantee the same thing this time. She hoped she would be lucky again and that the dream would not come true. She sighed, sitting on the tree stump before Chezuv showed up. She forgot he could read minds and she figured he had already read hers, so she knew there was no point telling him what was wrong. He looked at her with disappointment. That bugged her, so she finally asked.

"What! What is with the look of disappointment?" Akatila cried out.

"I understand that you have seen what is going to happen, but that does not mean you need to be pushing her away. You should be cherishing these times with her instead. Help her be excited, help her plan this. She is correct. It is a blessing that maybe everyone needs. After all the loss and battles we have dealt with lately; a wedding is a nice change. Maybe instead of trying to avoid what will happen, live in the moment like we all did a while back on the beach. You may lose her in a few months. Do you really want to lose her now?" Chezuv asked, looking down at her.

He left her sitting there deep in her thoughts. He only shook his head at her as he retreated to the fire pit where the others were beginning to talk about the wedding in a few months. Akatila could hear them laughing and talking. It only made her cringe even more. How was she supposed to be happy for her sister when she knew the truth, when she had a feeling that Yukia was not dead. She sighed. She also knew she couldn't tell anyone, mainly because she had no proof, and they would not believe her. She put her head in her hands and felt her body tense as she just wanted to cry. She knew she had to try and figure something out before she lost her sister for good. She wondered if maybe if she projected the memory she could figure out who takes her and where they go. She sighed, shaking her head. *"Someone might see what I cannot,"* she thought to herself. *"Time to face the music, Akatila, get up and act like you're super excited for her,"* she said softly to herself as she got up.

She entered the groups area quietly as everyone talked about the wedding. She looked for Angelia but did not see her. It made her heart race. Riku saw the look on Akatila's face and pointed to Shala's home. She gave him a smile and went toward the house before she was stopped by Harnuq.

"Maybe now is not the time to keep bringing your sister down," he growled.

"I just want to make this right," Akatila said coldly.

He growled but nodded to her and let her into the home. Angelia turned to see her sister and turned her back again. Akatila flinched a bit, but Shala left the tent quietly so they could talk.

"Hey, can we talk?" Akatila asked seeing Angelia by herself

"I suppose." She shrugged.

"I love you, Angelia, and I wish I could tell you what I know but I can't. But please trust me when I say this will not end well for you, you or Harnuq. Please, sis, just this once listen to me," Akatila pleaded.

Angelia looked at her sister with sadness and anger rising in her eyes. Akatila knew it was hopeless and she should just tell her what she wanted to hear. Chezuv was right, Akatila did not want to lose her sister and be on bad terms also. She had to fix this and act as if everything was okay and that she was happy for the wedding.

"I know you won't listen to me, you never have. Just know I am happy for you, and I look forward to seeing what dress you pick out next month. It must be as beautiful as you, Angelia, you deserve nothing less than the best." Akatila smiled, faking almost every word.

Angelia began to cry thinking her sister was on board. She hugged Akatila tightly and then ran off to tell Harnuq the great news. She could hear the cheers coming from the group. She knew that she had to protect her sister. Maybe this was the way. Maybe if she stuck by her sister's side she could prevent what was coming. She looked to the starry sky in hopes that their mother would help watch over Angelia during this time. She sighed, put on a fake smile, and went into the camp.

She walked into the camp just as they decided to bump up the wedding to a few days away. Akatila was slightly excited. Maybe that meant her fear would not come true. She hoped that if they upped the day of the wedding then her bad feeling would go away and what she saw could not happen as they would not know or have the time to prepare an attack like that. She finally smiled and hugged her sister tightly, thinking and hoping now she would be safe.

"Hey, why don't we get some sleep? Remember, tomorrow we are all going into town and getting stuff to prepare for the wedding, including your dress," Akatila reminded them.

Everyone nodded and went to sleep, except for Akatila. She stayed up all night. She was afraid to sleep. She did not want to see what could happen. She was exhausted when everyone woke up the next morning, but she played it off as if she were perfectly fine. Everyone made their way into the town excited to start shopping. The guys went one way while Shala,

Akatila, and Angelia went another way. The girls started with what type of food they wanted to serve. They tried a few different things, but Akatila decided to speak up.

"As my gift to you and Harnuq, why don't I bake everything? I am a really good cook," Akatila said proudly.

"Wait, really! You would do that for us?" Angelia replied.

Akatila nodded and Angelia gave her a huge hug before moving on to the next thing on the list. Akatila felt proud of her sister and excited to be helping where she could. She tried to listen to Chezuv and Malinter's advice to not push her away and pull her close instead before something did happen. They got excited knowing it was time to pick the material out for the wedding dress. Akatila knew her sister would go right for lace. Shala giggled and finally spoke up as well.

"You pick the material, Angelia, and I will make it for you," Shala said, smiling.

"You two are really the best!" Angelia said, giving Shala a hug.

She smiled to see her sister picking out the materials for her dress. She giggled to see that her sister was like a child picking out candy. Angelia looked over at Akatila and gave her a smile. They still had hardly spoken since the fight a few days ago but Angelia knew that Akatila was coming around to the thought as she was coming around her more often. They went farther into the town's market and found some beautiful flowers. Akatila rolled her eyes. She could not understand why her sister would want such dark colors at her wedding but she just shrugged.

"Come on, sis, what do you really think?" Angelia asked, looking at the flowers.

"Sorry, Angelia, I do not understand why you want such dark flowers. Shouldn't a wedding be light, bright, and amazing?" she asked, confused.

Angelia thought about it for a moment. She knew what her sister meant by the dark colors. She shook her head, putting the dark-colored roses down, and decided to go with the light pink, yellow, and soft, purple-colored roses instead.

Akatila smiled knowing she had helped with something for the wedding. She still was not convinced that the wedding should happen but she was happy for her sister. After everything they have been through, she knew her sister deserved to be happy and be in love and have a family. Akatila could not wait to have nieces and nephews. She just hoped her sister would make it to that day. She shook her head, realizing Angelia was snapping her fingers in front of her face.

"Huh? What?" Akatila said, shaking her head.

"Oh, never mind." Angelia sighed.

They went back to the camp and Shala began to discuss with Angelia where they wanted the wedding. She knew of a beautiful open field nearby. She also suggested where they first said, "I love you," which was by the ocean. Akatila thought about each one and how easy it would be for someone to hide and attack or how difficult. She knew if she were going to chime in on where the wedding would take place it had to be now.

"I think the field would be beautiful, but that is just my opinion," Akatila spoke up cheerfully.

"Do you think tomorrow will be good in a field?" Shala asked suspiciously.

"I think tomorrow would be a great day to have a wedding." Akatila replied.

"Tomorrow it is!" Angelia giggled.

Shala looked at her shocked, as did Angelia, except Angelia had a smile on her face as she thought Akatila was finally accepting that the wedding was going to happen no matter what. But Shala knew better. Shala knew there had to be another reason that Akatila would choose the field, she just did not know why. But she was going to find out exactly what was going on with Akatila. Shala wondered if maybe it was because Angelia decided to up the wedding date to tomorrow.

"You don't think that going from next year to tomorrow is a bit fast?" Shala asked Akatila.

"As long as she is happy." She replied.

The guys had shown back up talking about stuff. Angelia ran over to Harnuq and old him that tomorrow would be the day. He agreed as everyone grew excited.

"Thank you everyone who has helped us finalize everything these past few days. I could not be luckier to have a family such as this one. I will forever be grateful," Angelia said, speaking up.

"We want you to be happy, and tomorrow will be the best day of your life. We are so proud of how far you have come since you were little, Angelia. You went from a child to such a brave and beautiful young woman," Chezuv spoke first.

"And yet how in the world did you end up with a man like my brother?" Anoquv said jokingly.

"Trust me, when I find out I will let you know," Harnuq joked.

Everyone continued to talk but Akatila was lost in her thoughts. She could not shake the feeling that her fear would still happen. She shook her head and went down the stream to think. She sighed, placing her head in her hands. She felt helpless.

A hand was gently placed on her back. To her surprise it was Malinter. She looked at him shocked that he had come to her. She was hesitant to ask why.

"Chezuv told me about what you saw. Listen, I will do everything I can as well to help try to prevent it. But in the case we cannot prevent it, Akatila, you need to be ready, because we are not losing her. We lost you for a long time, we will not lose Angelia as well. You should get some rest. You are going to need your strength. The wedding is tomorrow, and if what you think will happen does happen, then the fight will be bad and you will need to be ready," he said, nodding to her as he returned to camp.

She knew he was right. She got to her feet and went back to camp to see everyone dancing and having a great time. She saw her sister smiling and she felt her heart break. She was not sure if tonight would be the last night she saw her sister. Tears came to her eyes, but she blinked quickly so no one saw them. After a little while, everyone went to bed to get ready for the big day. Akatila knew it would be a big day no matter what happened. She just wished everyone would be more on guard.

It was the day of the wedding, the day Akatila was dreading. She knew what today would bring, so she decided to do what she could to prevent that. She and Angelia were finally on talking terms again and back to being sisters. It was as if nothing had ever happened between them. She did not want to lose that. She began doing patrols as everyone else was setting up for the wedding. She found Raynier and Riku and pulled them to the side.

"Akatila, shouldn't you be getting ready for the wedding?" Riku asked as Raynier nodded in agreement.

"Listen, don't ask how I know this but something is wrong. I am not sure what but there is something off about today. Please keep an eye out," she said worriedly.

"Akatila, I just think you are nervous about the wedding. Your little sister is getting married, be happy," Raynier said, dismissing it. But Riku nodded.

She gave Riku a quick smile before vanishing into the shadows again, still doing her patrols. She just knew there had to be a way to stop this from happening. She heard the band strike up and she rushed to see her sister walk down the aisle. She saw Shala and Ze walking down. She watched as everyone stood up. Greto was holding on gently to Angelia's arm. Akatila smiled seeing her sister in a long lacy wedding dress. It fit her in all the right places but she still looked like a princess. Tears filled Akatila's eyes as she knew her little sister was no longer little. But she also knew the danger her sister was in and why. She watched and listened as Angelia and Harnuq exchanged vows and kissed. She was so proud of her sister and so excited for her new life—if she got to it.

Akatila saw something move by her quickly. She knew it was not Sprin as he was sitting down still. She decided to follow, and that was when she found her worst fear. She noticed it was Miko. He had a handful of soldiers running right to them all. She tried to get to everyone before he did. She tripped over almost everything. She knew even if she tried to yell for help no one would hear her, she was too far away still. She finally got to the bottom of the hill but it was too late. Miko reached them first and was creeping up on Shala and Angelia talking.

"We are so excited for you two. We wish you both all of the happiness in the world," Shala said softly to them.

Harnuq and Angelia smiled at her. Angelia looked up at Harnuq and felt her heart skip a few beats until she saw something. She narrowed her eyes, looking into the forest, and she finally saw him. She let out a screech before running away. Miko, Yukia, and a few soldiers had found them all. They charged at them as everyone scrambled. They were completely caught off guard. They thought Miko and Yukia were dead.

"Angelia, move!" Akatila cried, running down the hill to her sister.

It was too late. Miko had snatched her and run off into ShadowCry Forest. Akatila tried to follow him, but she kept getting hit by other soldiers. She growled, finally snapping and lashing out at the soldiers. She felt her panic getting the best of her. She finally broke free from the soldiers, only to end up getting attacked by Yukia. She could see Miko with her sister. She tried to go around Yukia but he would not let her pass.

"Yukia, move! I am not fighting you! We both know you cannot win against me, so just give up and let me go after my sister!" she spat.

"You think you can defeat me? I have had more training by Master Goenjo himself, you do not stand a chance. As for your sister, well, let us just say that you will never find her. You will never see her again. And you saw this coming but there was nothing you could do," Yukia snickered.

She knew he was right. When she looked over her shoulder, she saw everyone standing there. Harnuq was furious and heartbroken. He glared at Akatila. She knew he had heard Yukia but at the time she did not care, she only wanted her sister.

She snapped her gaze back to Yukia, who had shifted into his fox. She shifted into her leopard. She let him make the first move. He ran at her full speed; she did not move. She had her eyes closed. When she snapped her eyes open, she ducked under him but used her teeth, clamping onto his leg, stopping him from going over her. She whipped him around by his leg. He let out yowls and growls as she threw him to the ground. She let go of his leg knowing he could not run this time.

Chezuv watched from the shadows and tried to keep other soldiers off her and Yukia. She shifted back to herself, as did Yukia, who was screaming in pain as his leg was bleeding badly. She shifted back into her fox. She dashed off, leaving everyone standing there. She got to the hill where she last saw her sister and found the dolphin necklace on the ground. She then saw the sky was orange and knew that meant a fire somewhere. Yukia used the moment that everyone was running off to escape, he knew his time would be now. He slipped away despite his injury to Miko. Miko nodded as they made their way with Angelia to a small town that they knew would draw Akatila.

CHAPTER FIFTEEN

She stood there silently as she looked around. She could smell fire from a distance and her heart sank. She knew the winds were blowing from the east. As her first home, where her family had lived before the war, was to the east, she put her hand to her heart and sighed. A hand was placed on her shoulder. She turned to see Riku with the others and Raynier removed his hand.

"I am sorry about your home, sweets." he said softly to her.

She shook her head as she looked to Harnuq. He looked at her confused before he looked at Akatila's hand. She was holding the dolphin charm Harnuq had carved for Angelia. Akatila's eyes filled with tears, she fell to her knees. Raynier was right beside her, holding her as she just cried. Harnuq stood there in disbelief. He shook his head and went to run toward the town, but his brother grabbed him and pulled him to the ground.

"Harnuq, she's gone! I am sorry, but she is gone. There is nothing we can do for her now," Anoquv said, trying to fight back the tears.

"No!" Harnuq cried out as he tried to fight off his brother.

Akatila cried as she stumbled to Harnuq. She placed her hand on his shoulder. He calmed down for a moment. As she placed the carving in his hands, he finally broke. He began to sob, staring at it. He could hear her voice the day he gave it to her. Harnuq let the memory flow.

"Harnuq, where are you taking me?" Angelia giggled, following Harnuq.

"I can't tell you, it's a surprise. One you will love, I promise," he replied, holding her hand, guiding her.

They got to the ocean. Angelia smiled looking out across the sea. The sun was just setting so the sky was an orange pink, making the water look purple in the distance. She took a deep breath, taking in the saltwater smell. She felt Harnuq wrap his arms around her from behind. She swayed side to side with him for a moment before she turned to face him. He adjusted his hands, gently placing them on her waist.

"Was this the surprise? It's beautiful, Harnuq." She smiled up at him.

"No, this is," he said, pulling a little wooden carving out of his pocket. Angelia looked down to see a wooden dolphin carving. She gave a huge smile as she giggled. It was painted a beautiful dark gray while its eyes were a dark blue. He watched her as she slowly took it from him and attached it to her necklace.

"Now you have a piece of me with you as well. I know your sister gave you the original necklace, so I just made a tagalong for it," he said, blushing.

"I love it! Thank you. I love you," she said shyly.

"What?" he said, unsure about the last part of her sentence.

"I . . . um . . . well . . . I love you," Angelia repeated.

"I love you too." He kissed her softly before sitting down with her on the sand and watching the sun continue to set.

He snapped out of the memory feeling his brother shake him. Harnuq looked around and Akatila was gone. Chezuv stepped forward from the shadows, looking down at him. He knelt, placing his hand gently on Harnuq's back.

"We have a problem. While you were daydreaming, Akatila went to the town to see if she could find Angelia. She's been gone too long," Chezuv said, standing back up.

The others had already gone. Harnuq only saw his brother and Chezuv. He shifted into his timber wolf knowing it would be a long run and it would be easier in his other form. He waited for the others. He knew this would be another fight.

Shala bowed her head to Chezuv also understanding the same thing. She began gathering herbs as she was not fully sure what to expect. She was the only one to remain in human form. Riku, Raynier, Seto, Harnuq, Anoquv, Ze, Malinter, and Sprin all shifted, and each one took off at different times.

Raynier thought to himself, *I hope she does not do anything reckless.* He shook his head and focused on running after everyone.

Chezuv knew that Raynier and Riku were both worried, so was he.

They got to the village entrance and saw many of the houses and businesses on fire. People were still trying to get out of the village and to a safe distance. Chezuv shifted back to himself, as did everyone else.

"Before we go looking for Akatila we have to set up a safe base. Shala, get whatever herbs you may need. You are going to have a lot of burned victims, maybe even children. If you think it could be a possibility, then grab it," Chezuv said to her.

"I will. Ze, help me with this," she said to him softly.

Shala and Ze quickly cleared an area just outside of the village. Shala began to take count of what she had and what she was missing. She made sure that the tables were clean and enough for plenty of people to be able to lie down and rest. She counted herbs twice as fast as she could just to be safe. Ze ran down to the nearby stream and got plenty of water. Shala looked to Ze with worry in her eyes as she realized she did not have enough herbs.

"Ze, I don't have enough to help everyone, I need more," she said, heartbroken.

"Okay, well, what do you need? I can go find some," he said, assuring her.

"I need chamomile, milk thistle, mullein leaf, hops, and peppermint. I have plenty of everything else," she said carefully.

He nodded and ran off into the thicket and began grabbing what he could find. He also knew that people had been inhaling the smoke and they would need more clean water to try and help. He also knew Shala might need extra water to clean off wounds. Ze placed the herbs beside the others for Shala before grabbing the few jugs he found. He ran to the stream and filled each of the jugs up. He put some jugs down by the table and stood guard waiting. He knew this was going to be a long day and there was going to be much loss. He just hoped Angelia would not be among the dead.

"Seto, you and Malinter, each of you will go into four houses down in the southern part of town. Raynier, you and Riku will take four houses on the east side. Anoquv and Harnuq, four house in the west. Sprin, you and I will take the northern part of town, four houses. Once you are done with that meet right back here. Greto, you stay here and direct people as they come out towards Shala and Ze. Then we go look for Akatila," he said sternly.

Everyone nodded in agreement and went the way they were told.

Greto, Shala and Ze stood there. Ze gently held on to her as they all prepared for the worst.

Everyone went their separate ways to try and save more people. Seto and Malinter had gone to the south part of the town where they came to a small shop with the innkeeper was pinned down by some beams. Seto ran over and started clearing the debris off him while Malinter went straight for some of the smaller beams. They got to the bigger beam holding him down and lifted together. Seto helped the man from under it. Malinter led the man back to Shala while Seto continued to the last two houses. Finding both empty, he returned to Malinter, and they waited for the others.

Raynier and Riku went east. To their surprise the eastern part of town was not on fire yet, so they were able to evacuate everyone to Shala and Ze. They stood beside Malinter and Seto waiting patiently.

Anoquv and Harnuq went west and came to find that the area had been evacuated and was not on fire. They both looked at each other in confusion.

"How can the south and north sides be on fire but the west and east are not?" Riku asked, puzzled.

"I am not sure, Riku, but I am sure we will find out," Raynier replied.

They both returned and waited with the others. All that was left was Chezuv and Sprin, who were emerging from the north with a few people behind them. Shala dropped everything and ran to them, taking some of the children as everyone remained silent. They looked to Chezuv, who was waiting by the entrance to the village. Chezuv did not shift, so they all knew that it would be better to do this in human form in case they ran across any more survivors.

They took off back through the village searching for Akatila. At first they had no idea where to even begin looking for her. She could be anywhere in the town. Then they found another home on fire with people still trapped inside. They all shifted back into themselves and looked at the house in horror. Chezuv and Malinter ran around the back to try and break through. Anoquv and Harnuq tried to tear down the debris in front of the door blocking their way inside. Raynier ran back and got Shala. He knew that they would not be able to get everyone to her without losing someone. He brought Ze and Shala back to the house.

"Ze, how are they supposed to get in?" Shala

"I think I can see a way in, but it's a small hole. None of us will fit there," he replied, looking at the door.

"I can get in there," Akatila said, appearing beside them.

Ze said nothing as he was in shock. He had no idea where she came from, but as quickly as she came, she was gone. She dove right into the small hole and wandered around looking for anyone to get out. She noticed the house was on fire but she noticed it was not as bad as the other homes. She shrugged it off and began searching each room carefully. She was unsure where any survivors could be, but she knew she was not going to give up. She heard some beams crack. She glanced up in time to see them breaking and about to fall. She ran forward a bit. The broken beams fell behind her, sending some pieces of the flaming wood onto her, making her jump away even more. She brushed off the pieces and went back to her task.

She finally heard some noise coming from a room; however, the house was now fully on fire. She saw debris falling from the ceiling and from the sides of the house. *Crap, I need to pick up my pace,"* she told herself.

She dodged the debris from the burning house. She knew it was going to be a tight fit as she came to a dead end. She growled and dug into the debris. The soft wood made it easy to make a hole for herself and get through to the other side where she knew there were people. She shifted into herself so no one saw her as she approached the room of people.

"Okay, is everyone okay?" she asked, counting the people.

"Yes, we are all here and okay, just scared," replied a young man.

"Alright, follow me and stay close. I will get you out of here and to safety," Akatila said, helping everyone to their feet.

She led them out of the doorway and back toward the hole she had made earlier. She counted as everyone went through it to the other side where Anoquv and Harnuq were waiting. She felt someone pull on her pants and she looked down to see a little girl with big green eyes and curly brown hair staring up at her. She knelt out of curiosity. She did not know what this child wanted, maybe to be carried through the hole.

"My sister and mommy are somewhere back there. They forgot about her because we are twins and twins are bad. But Mommy went looking for her," the little girl said softly.

"Do you know where?" Akatila asked softly.

"No, I just know they forgot her on purpose. Please, I am sure she is scared without her teddy bear," she replied.

Akatila noticed the burnt teddy bear the little girl was holding and knew that Angelia would want her to find this child first. Akatila nodded as she picked her up and handed her to Anoquv before turning away and going back to look for the child. She shifted into her fox and decided to try and look for the woman and the missing child.

She stopped at every house and looked but there was no sign of them. Then she heard something. Akatila stopped dead in her tracks as she heard something. She twitched her ears as she tried to pinpoint what the noise was and where it was coming from. Her ears perked as she heard it again and she dashed off, her claws digging into the ground to gain better traction and speed. She was not sure what she was running into but she knew it was a child. She slowed down as the cry got louder. She shifted back to herself and walked around the corner, where she saw a house burning. Standing outside the house crying was a young mom covered in burns and blood holding a burnt teddy bear. *That perhaps belongs to the other three- or four-year-old little girl,* Akatila thought. She quickly noticed there was no baby with the young woman.

"Is everyone okay? We need to get you out of here," she said calmly but quickly.

"My baby! My baby!" the women cried out, pointing to the house.

Akatila's eyes grew wide. She looked back at the burning house and her heart sank. There was no way this lady meant her baby was still in the house they were just in. Akatila saw Seto and Malinter show up. She nodded to them as she ran into the house. She coughed from the smoke. The house was bigger than she remembered. She looked around but could barely see anything due to the smoke. She was glad not to see any flames yet. She ran back outside to Seto and Malinter. She did not see the mother or the other child. She glanced at Seto.

"We took them to Shala. The mother said her baby was in the back with some other people. Akatila, did you see anyone else in the house?" Seto said calmly.

"No, but I also could not get around to the back half, some debris blocked my way. There has to be another way into this house," she replied.

"Hey, you two, back here!" Malinter called from the back side of the house.

"It is not big enough to get everyone out. If I can get in maybe I can find a way out or make a way out," she said quickly as she started climbing through an exceedingly small hole.

All they could do was hope she was right in doing this, they knew they could not keep her from trying. Seto ran back to the front to see if he could find a way in while Malinter looked over the sides to see if there was a weak spot. Malinter sighed softly as he could not find another way into the house. Then he heard something begin to crack. He snapped his head up to the oak tree that was on fire beside the house. He ran away from the side as the tree trunk was beginning to break. He watched from a distance as it finally broke, sending the massive tree down on the house. Malinter ran back to see if it had hit anyone, and by nothing but luck it missed everyone and crashed into a tiny room. He saw Seto and he sighed with relief seeing he was able to get though and get into the house. He and Seto began moving the debris so Akatila could have a clear path. They were done and could only wait for her.

Akatila could feel the flames get hotter and hotter the farther she went into the house. She coughed as she felt like her lungs were also on fire. She could not see much, so she shifted into her fox and tried to use her small-framed animal form to get below the cloud of smoke forming. She cried out in hopes that someone would hear her and call out for help. Akatila noticed there was a secret part to the house. She was about to give up hope when she came to a blocked door at the very back of the house. She shifted to herself knowing this had to be the spot where everyone was. She moved the debris and managed to swing the door open to reveal a room full of small children and one burnt-up young woman. She helped the woman to her feet along with a few of the children. She managed to get them to Malinter and Seto before nodding to them. They knew she was going back into the house to get the rest, Akatila could not live with herself if she left the other children behind.

Akatila rushed back into the burning house and was able to get some people out. She grabbed the baby she could hear crying and ran out. She found the mom, who was crying for her child. Akatila smiled, revealing the baby was safe. Shala rushed over to check the baby, who was luckily unharmed. Akatila saw Riku and Raynier rush in as well. She and Seto were next once they came out, but they never did.

"Seto, they have been in there a while. What if—" She began to panic.

"Come on, we will go look. You go left and I will go right," Seto said quickly.

She nodded and followed her brother into the fire. He went right and she went left. She crashed into some horses trying to get out. She felt one of them trample her leg. She screamed but she knew no one could hear her over the raging flames. She growled in pain and popped her leg back into place. She cried out again. She took a moment to breathe and then tried to get up. She was able to get up but she knew she needed to get out.

She saw Chezuv with Malinter fighting people. She shifted into her fox and charged but got hit from the side. It was another fox and she knew who it was, Yukia. She snarled, leaping at the fox, pinning it down. She dug her claws into the fox's shoulder, making it yelp in pain. The other fox shifted and it in fact was Yukia. He smirked at her and pulled a piece of broken wood and stabbed her in the paw with it, causing her to let him go. She shifted back to herself, seeing her hand bleeding. She ran after Yukia. She grabbed a cloth as he ran farther into the fire. She placed it over her nose and mouth to help her breathe.

"Great, where did he go?" she coughed.

She looked around but then heard someone calling for her. She knew she had to get her leg and hand checked. She turned back and saw Seto waiting for her. She coughed again as he helped her out of the smoke. They were greeted by Chezuv and Shala. Shala quickly dressed the wound on her hand before even noticing her leg. She gasped at seeing her leg and ran back for other herbs.

"I saw him! He is here! Yukia, he has to be the one behind everything!" Akatila stammered.

"Where? Where did you see him, Akatila?" Chezuv asked calmly.

"I am not sure, there was too much smoke everywhere to be able to tell where we were. All I know is I went to help you and Malinter with that fight and he attacked me. He came from the shadows, and just as quickly as he attacked me, he went farther into the flames," she replied, shaking.

Everyone became on edge knowing that this fire that they thought was an accident was a setup but no one knew why. Chezuv, Malinter, and Sprin stepped to the side while Seto was getting checked out by Shala. Akatila looked for everyone and noticed that people were missing.

"Where are they?" She asked turning to Ze.

"They went back in the fire to make sure everyone was out." Ze replied unsure.

"Why aren't they back yet?" she cried out.

She did not wait for a response, she leaped away and dove into the fire. Seto shook Shala off him and ran after his sister. He found her coughing looking for them. He nudged her pointing he would go one way and she would go the other. She nodded and they split up.

"Raynier!" Seto called out coughing.

"Riku!" Akatila cried out.

She began to lose hope when someone caught her eye. The person ran off, she thought it was her sister. It looked like her, so she chased after the person. She ducked under some broken beams and ended up stumbling out of the house into the clearing. The person seemed to be waiting for her. Akatila stumbled after the person as they ran off again.

"Hey! Wait!" she called out.

She followed the stranger until she came to a barn that had just begun to burn. She coughed from breathing in all the smoke. She shook her head quickly. She then heard someone call out. She looked up from the ground. She looked around but she did not see anyone. She became confused

"Hello?" she called out as she entered the burning barn.

Akatila frantically looked around. She knew she had to be here somewhere, there was nowhere else anyone could have taken her. She heard a small whimper come from the back right corner. Akatila made a mad dash to the corner, only to find a small child. She sighed in despair. She gently picked up the little girl and walked back out.

There was still smoke everywhere but she was able to find her way back to the group and to Shala. Shala saw Akatila first and then saw she was carrying something. To Shala's surprise it was a small child. She ran over to them with relief and confusion.

"Um, Akatila, where did this child come from?" Shala asked, confused.

"I found her in the barn in the corner just crying. She was alone but it looks like she has a few wounds. Can you help her while I find the others?" she asked, gently placing the child down.

"Of course," Shala replied softly.

"She will take care of you until I come back. Stay here," she said softly to her. "Will you be good for her?" Akatila asked sweetly.

The little girl nodded but remained silent, Akatila sighed softly as she got back to her feet. Shala nodded and Akatila turned, facing the smoke again. She knew her friends were in there and so was her sister. She had no choice but to find them. She put her cloth over her mouth and nose and went back into the burning village. She coughed from the smoke but she spotted someone.

She ran after them, only as she got closer did she realize who it was. She sighed in relief to see Riku with Raynier trying to put out some of the smaller fires. She let them be as they had not seen her yet. She went farther into the village. She figured she was in the town market by now. She saw a few small kids again. *"Where are these children coming from?"* she thought to herself. She went toward them but someone beat her to it.

"Akatila, get back. This part of the village is on fire still, there is no way to get in yet. Ze is flying overhead to find a way in," Chezuv said as he gently picked up the two children.

She nodded and turned back. She saw a different way and decided to try that path. She saw someone run and she shifted into her fox to try and keep up. She dodged some falling debris but kept coughing from the smoke. She looked around a little lost and dazed from not being able to get a good breath of air. She shook her head and staggered a bit but she remained on her paws. She saw the person again and wondered why they kept running. She growled to herself and followed them. She then noticed after running a bit that they were running out of the village. Akatila came to a stop and shifted back to herself, looking at the person. The person stopped as well before bowing their head to her and retreating into the shadows. Akatila was left standing there lost, confused, and exhausted. She groaned as she looked around. *"Great, lost again,"* she thought to herself.

"Do not be mad," a voice came from the shadows.

"Angelia?" Akatila said slowly.

"No, Angelia is not here but I am. You are Akatila Ray, aren't you? Sister to Angelia and Seto, daughter of Greto," the voice answered.

Akatila at first was hesitant to reply. She was not sure how someone knew that. She did not recognize that voice, so she knew it was not her sister or any of her friends. She growled, taking a step back figuring, this was another trap set up by Yukia and Miko. A small-figured woman stepped out of the shadows. She was covered in black clothing with only a little bit of blue laced into the material of her kimono. The woman would not look up from the ground. Her voice was slightly familiar to Akatila but she did not know why.

"You are looking for your sister, correct?" the woman spoke softly again.

"Yes, have you seen her? She looks just like me. Please, I need to find her. We are all worried about her," Akatila replied.

"I can take you to her, but after that can you answer a few questions for me?" she asked.

"Yes, of course, just please take me to my sister," Akatila begged the woman.

The lady nodded and walked off into the shadows. Akatila went to step forward, but she could hear everyone calling for her. They sounded worried as well. She whistled, letting them know she was okay and where she was. Chezuv and Malinter were the first to get to her, followed by Harnuq, Anoquv, Ze, and Sprin. Seto, Greto, and Shala were the last to arrive as Seto was still being bandaged by Shala.

"I saw someone. She knows where Angelia is. But her voice, Chezuv, I am not sure, but I have heard it before," Akatila said, puzzled.

"Akatila, I cannot tell you not to follow that woman, I just ask you to be careful. We are not sure if Angelia is there or not. Ze, can you fly overhead in the distance and keep an eye out for any other danger?" Chezuv said, turning to him.

"Of course, Chezuv. I will stay out of sight but also keep Akatila in my sights," he replied calmly.

"It is settled then. Akatila, do what you must. But be warned, we will not be far behind you. I will not lose you also," Harnuq said, stepping forward.

"We second that!" Riku and Raynier both chimed in.

Akatila let out a soft giggle before walking to Riku. She placed her hand gently on his face before looking to Raynier with a smile. She turned and followed the strange woman. Ze shifted and flew off. There was a moment of silence before Greto finally spoke up.

"She is about to learn the truth, isn't she? That woman, Chezuv, is it who I think it is?" he said hopefully.

"I do believe so, but I am not sure what Master Goenjo has done to her or the king. Do not forget about him. Just because we have not dealt with him yet does not mean we can forget he still holds the ace to this war," Chezuv warned.

Akatila ducked under some branches that had fallen. She figured it was from the fires. The woman continued down into ShadowCry Forest, in which Akatila knew every path. But this was a path she had never been down before. When she came out of the forest, she was standing in front of a well-built house. She shook her head as a flashback came rushing to her.

"Come on, Akatila! Walk to me, that's my girl!" a woman said, smiling.

Akatila shook her head again, almost falling over. She gasped for air as the memories would not stop flooding her mind. She looked at the door to the house and it had her family's crest on it. She looked at her arm and it was a perfect match.

"Seto, leave your sisters alone!" a woman said.

"Aw, but Mom!" he replied.

"Do not 'but' your mother, young man!" a man's voice boomed.

She knew those voices. The young boy was Seto and the man was Greto. She looked at the woman, who had opened the door. Angelia was standing there in the courtyard. Angelia was holding something. When she turned around, Akatila saw it was a small teddy bear. Akatila ran to her sister in tears. She crashed into Angelia, holding on to her. Angelia cried into Akatila's shoulder.

"Angelia, where did you go? Why did you not come back? Where are we? Harnuq has been a mess without you," Akatila began to ramble.

"I wanted to come back, I couldn't. Miko had me captive. I could not figure out where he had taken me. Once I broke free, I was lost. I ran for hours trying to figure out where you guys were. When I did find the camp, it was empty. It looked like you guys had left. I got into some fights and then she found me. She brought me here. Akatila, this is our home, the place before the other house," Angelia said quickly.

"Who's she?" Akatila finally asked, looking to the lady.

"You were truly little the day it happened. We were all separated. General Miko and Master Goenjo had taken me from you all. I missed you so much. I am so proud of how you three grew up," she said softly.

"Three?" Akatila questioned.

She noticed everyone had shown up and were standing by the door, including Seto and Greto. Greto looked as if he had been crying. His gaze never left the strange woman. Seto looked as if he wanted to cry as well. Akatila looked to her sister in confusion, but Angelia was being held by Harnuq. She let out a small giggle and looked back at the woman. She glanced at Greto. He nodded to her. Seto nodded as well, but she noticed no one moved forward.

"How do you know about us? Who are you?" she demanded.

"Akatila," she said gently.

The woman removed all the black clothing, revealing gentle brown eyes; long, curly brown hair being held back by a beautiful butterfly pin. Her kimono was white laced with blue and purple. Green trimmed the ends of the sleeves and along the bottom of the kimono. She revealed her arm, which had the family crest as well.

Akatila stood there shocked. She knew those eyes but she could not figure out why. She glanced back at her sister, and the look on Angelia's face told her. Seto let out a small sigh of relief. The silence could easily be sliced with a knife. It was dead silent. She snapped her gaze back to the woman in shock. She staggered backward in confusion but she felt hands gentle on her waist. She looked back and it was Riku smiling at her. She knew she had to ask the question, but fear gripped her along with rising anger. Riku helped her relax as she could feel his hands still gentle on her. She took a deep breath and finally got the courage to ask.

"Mom?" she stammered.

CPSIA information can be obtained
at www.ICGtesting.com
Printed in the USA
BVHW032334140621
609529BV00012B/2481/J

9 781664 178281